SNACKS, SCHEDULES, AND EVERYONE'S A SUSPECT

A CARLINE COZY MYSTERY

KRISTIN ELIZABETH

Snacks, Schedules, and Everyone's a Suspect

This work is a human-authored creation. No generative artificial intelligence (AI) was used in the writing or production of this work.

This is a work of fiction/non-fiction. Names, characters, places, and incidents are products of the author's imagination or are used fictitiously.

Cover Created by: Eden Cheung

Book Formatted by: Josephine Carnes, Treasure Trove PA (@treasuretrovepa)

First Edition: May 2026

Ebook ISBN 979-8-234-09108-6

ISBN 979-8-234-09109-3

Published by:

Thunder & Ink

@ThunderandInk

This book is for tired moms everywhere who spend so much time taking care of everyone else that they sometimes forget who they are beneath the schedules, snacks, and endless mental checklists.

I hope this story reminds you that you are still in there. Still funny. Still smart. Still worthy of adventures, friendships, joy, and a life that belongs to you.

And if you happen to solve a murder along the way, even better.

CONTENTS

ACKNOWLEDGMENTS

Writing this book was equal parts exciting, terrifying, and slightly chaotic, which feels fitting for a story centered around carline moms and murder.

First, thank you to Kenny, who patiently listened to me talk and talk and talk about this project as it ever so gradually became a real book. Thank you for encouraging me, supporting me, and pretending not to mind when every casual conversation somehow circled back to the story I was trying to create.

To Lennon, thank you for changing the way I see the world. So much of this story exists because of you. Your joy, your struggles, and the way you notice things others miss inspired more of this book than you will ever probably realize.

To Elaine, my sounding board, continuity queen, and voice of reason, thank you for helping me keep all the moving pieces together. Every writer needs someone who can say, "Wait… didn't this happen three chapters ago?" and somehow still make them feel sane afterward.

To Josephine at Treasure Trove PA, for editing and formatting support. Because of you, this story became something readers can finally hold in their hands.

Finally, thank you to every reader who took a chance on a cozy mystery about carlines, motherhood, friendship, and murder. I'm so glad you're here. And I hope you'll come back.

CHAPTER 1
MONDAY | CARLINE

IF THERE WERE a competitive sport for surviving an elementary school carline, Madison Carter, or as her friends called her, Maddie, would have at least medaled on sheer endurance alone.

Warren Baldwin was Dogwood Bay's only elementary school, serving about four hundred students. The town itself sat along the Mississippi River, though these days the water was more background scenery than a source of community pride.

Once a growing river town, Dogwood Bay had settled into something quieter. Named for the pink and white dogwood trees lining its streets, it was an affordable suburban pocket surrounded by a few struggling farms and a small industrial park that employed much of the town's blue-collar workforce.

Most people in Dogwood Bay had lived there their entire lives, but Maddie's family was an exception. They had moved from St. Louis two years earlier, bringing their remote jobs with them. Maddie worked in marketing, and Kent was a mortgage underwriter. It wasn't a poor community, but in a town where most families relied on one income and few kids

rode the bus, routines mattered, and everyone knew everyone.

All this ultimately meant that the carline wasn't just a carline. It was so much more.

It was where things happened. Where plans were made. And where secrets unfolded.

Drop-off. Pick-up. Quick conversations that turned into long ones. A place to catch up, compare notes, and quietly keep tabs on everyone else.

A place to watch.

And, more than occasionally, judge.

Maddie was a people watcher. Not out of curiosity, but necessity. Her schedule didn't leave room for small talk, and she preferred it that way.

In and out. Efficient and invisible whenever possible.

She eased her blue sedan into the carline queue, already ten cars deeper than she liked, and glanced at the clock. 8:35 a.m.

"Let's moooove," she murmured. "Ya'll have it so easy. Just put it in park and let 'em jump out."

Maddie took schedules more seriously than others and prayed she would never be late for drop-off. Latecomers had to park and drop their child off at the school office. It came with a huge loss of time, time that Maddie didn't have to spare.

From the backseat, Lennon made a loud humming noise, the same one he made when he was content, or overstimulated, or somewhere in between. Maddie had long since stopped trying to categorize it. She felt as though his verbal stims were just... Lennon. They didn't always have to *mean* something. They just were.

"Hey, buddy," she said, glancing at him in the rearview mirror. "We made it."

"Mum." That one simple word brought a smile to her face. Lennon was nine, autistic, and still trying to find his voice.

She exhaled, eyes closed, just for a second. Just a second to reset. The kind of second that felt too long and too short, but also necessary.

Her phone buzzed in the cupholder.

A client.

Of course it was. Regardless of how many times she reiterated that she was only available by text from 10 to 3, her clients continued to reach out whenever they wanted.

Maddie cracked one eye open, read the preview: *"Quick edit request. Shouldn't take long!"*

"Nothing takes 'not long,'" she whispered, dropping her head dramatically and with unintended force onto the horn.

HONK.

The sound blasted through the quiet carline like a foghorn.

Maddie jerked upright so fast she nearly whiplashed herself. "Crap."

She sat there, teeth clenched, slapping a hand over the center of the wheel, telling it to be quiet, like that might undo what had just happened.

Too late.

Every head in the school's radius turned.

Including Vanessa. The woman idling directly in front of her.

Put together. Oversized sunglasses covering a third of her face. The kind of posture that suggested she was a pageant queen in her youth and was still hoping for world peace. She wasn't overdone, but impeccable, planned. Like she was trying to avoid attention, but instead, commanded it.

Vanessa Sams, Ellie's mom, member of the third-grade group chat.

Vanessa turned slowly, deliberately, and looked straight at Maddie.

Not confused. Not startled. Just... assessing. Almost a glare, but not quite unfriendly enough to be deemed so.

Maddie gave a tight, apologetic wave, miming "sorry" with her lips.

Vanessa didn't wave back, but offered a simple nod of acknowledgment. She sat watching Maddie for a moment too long before turning forward again.

"Great," Maddie muttered. "Love that for me."

From the sidewalk, Miss Merissa appeared; the rest of Lennon's class was waiting with their classroom aide, Evan. Evan was a twenty-something college student working towards a degree in education. Lennon adored both of them. Miss Merissa rushed to the car to greet Lennon and walk him to his classmates. She did so with efficiency and joy.

"Lennon!" she called brightly, opening the car door before singing, "Good morning!"

Maddie reached behind her to help unbuckle her son and hand off his backpack and lunch as Miss Merissa beamed at Lennon.

"Bye, buddy." Maddie waved.

"Bye, Mom, bye," he responded. Lennon slid out of the car without rushing. He paused briefly at the door, always the pause, then stepped out of the car, ready to walk away with his teacher.

"Hi, Lennon," she said warmly. "Let's have a great day today."

Maddie smiled, grateful as always for the lack of hesitation in his teacher's voice. "Thank you," she sighed. "We'll take all the great days we can get."

Miss Merissa laughed. "Don't we all."

The door shut, and just like that, the car was lighter. Quieter.

Maddie sat back, exhaling again, this time a little less dramatically. Around her, carline life continued. The childless wait for parents to turn left out of the school drop-off lane felt even longer than the drop-off itself.

Three cars up, Donna, the wannabe PTA President, was half out of her SUV window, talking to someone in the parking lot like the line wasn't actively moving. The school didn't even have a PTA; she was just the type of person Maddie imagined in that role.

Donna Taft, Laura's mom, founding member of the third-grade group chat.

She was involved in everything: fundraisers and school plays, thank-you gifts to the teachers and crossing guards, and she was ALWAYS in the principal's ear about something.

With Donna, her presence was known, just the way she wanted it. From the click-clacking of her heels to the scent of her coconut-infused hairspray, you knew she was coming even before she arrived. Donna loved attention, and it was apparent in the way she acted and looked, with perfectly coiffed hair and a wardrobe that matched head to toe.

She was basically the opposite of Maddie, who wore a disheveled pixie cut and, most days, sweats. Her makeupless face was a stark contrast to the lash extensions she treated herself to twice a month.

Behind Maddie, a dad she'd only ever seen at drop-off, never pick-up, was scrolling his phone, per usual, while he waited not-so-patiently to exit the carline.

Derek Holloway, Sara's dad, member of the third-grade group chat.

The bus line formed its own type of ecosystem. Kids exited the bus, backpacks bigger than their torsos, while a handful of teachers attempted to maintain order with limited success. The phrase herding cats always came to mind as Maddie observed from her car.

Her gaze drifted back to Vanessa, one car length in front of her.

"What's your story?" she wondered aloud.

Sunglasses still on. Hands at ten and two. Not moving, even as the line inched forward.

Something about her felt off. She was too collected; she moved with too much purpose, too much intent. Especially considering they were in an elementary school carline.

Like she wasn't just waiting.

Like she was watching.

Tracking something.

Or someone.

The cars came to a halt. Vanessa turned in her seat, another look in Maddie's direction with a sympathetic smile on her face. Maddie noticed the woman grab an emerald green notebook from her dashboard, jot something down, then discard it in her passenger seat before breaking the gaze and turning back around.

Maddie blinked. "What was that? What's she writing in there?" she asked no one but herself.

Carline moved again. Vanessa pulled forward, precise and measured, stopping exactly where she needed to without any hesitation.

Maddie followed, waiting for her turn.

Her phone buzzed again, but she ignored it this time.

Looking behind her, Maddie saw Miss Merissa guiding students inside, smiling, waving, and somehow managing to keep everything running without losing her mind.

Maddie envied that. Deeply. She was always losing her mind. Always.

She glanced up once more at Vanessa's SUV.

Maddie shook her head lightly, focusing instead on traffic and making her way out of the lot without causing another scene.

"Get it together," she murmured. "She's just... specific... detail-oriented. You take notes, too."

Maddie took notes because, at times, her brain felt like mush, and without them, she would no doubt forget something.

She couldn't help but wonder if Vanessa had written something about her. Those looks, irritation, or maybe pity, were making Maddie feel uncomfortable (and maybe a little guilty) even though she hadn't really done anything wrong, other than an accidental honk of the horn.

The carline moved again.

The same parents, the same kids, the same teachers that Maddie saw every morning.

Nothing out of the ordinary. At least not much.

People seemed to be running later than usual, but it was a Monday, after all.

Maddie thought back to the emerald green notebook.

That wasn't out of the ordinary, but it was a bit...

Strange.

CHAPTER 2
MONDAY | FUEL

BY 9:12 A.M., Maddie had already lived what felt like an entire day.

Drop-off chaos.

One mildly judgmental parent.

Two ignored client messages.

And a breakfast consisting of exactly three bites of a protein bar she discovered in her car, only slightly melted from the sun.

She pulled into the drive-thru of U-Brewed, her go-to, and rolled her window down.

U-Brewed was one of her favorite spots in town, right along the river walk. Other people came for the free internet, coffee specials, and good vibes, but Maddie came for the caffeine alone.

The speaker crackled. "U-Brewed! What can we get started for you?"

"An Iced Passion Energy," she stated. "Make it a large." After a brief pause, she added, "And with Strawberry Boba."

"We can do that. $6.95."

"Thank you."

She pulled forward, drumming her fingers against the

steering wheel, her brain seemingly miles away. Once again, feeling like a hamster on a wheel, just going through the motions of the day, while making very little progress. Just like she did every. Single. Day.

She was in a rut.

Emails.
Client edits.
Laundry.
Appointments.

The same day played on repeat, time and time again. Somewhere, over the last few years, she had lost herself a bit and, for lack of a better word, she was bored.

She glanced at the empty backseat and exhaled.

Quiet.

She loved Lennon more than anything, but the silence after drop-off always hit the same way. Relief wrapped in guilt.

Her phone buzzed.

Tara
I see you. 👀 Don't ignore me like you did in carline.

Maddie snorted. Peering through the parking lot for Tara's car.

Maddie
Ignore YOU? Impossible..

Tara
What was up with the 📢 aggressive honking?

Maddie
It was not aggressive.

Tara
▶▶You honked at VANESSA.

Meet me inside.

Five minutes later, Maddie, along with her drive-thru order, stepped into the cool, overly aesthetic interior of the coffee shop, where everything was a little retro, a lot curated, and probably designed for the sole purpose of being Instagrammable.

Tara was perched at a high top, her phone charging beside her.

Tara Hoffner, Piper's mom, member of the third-grade group chat, and Maddie's best friend.

Tara had straight, straw blonde hair and blue eyes. Her lilac sunglasses perched atop her head, and a smile that could rival Julia Roberts's. Her drink had no business being called coffee, and honestly, with all the sugar and creamer Tara added, Maddie wasn't so sure it even was anymore.

"You're late," Tara said, not looking up from her phone.

"I've already had a full emotional arc today," Maddie replied, sliding into the chair across from her. "I honestly forgot we were meeting up; you're lucky I made it at all."

They sat for a moment in comfortable silence. Both exhaling the chaos of the morning carline as they sipped their drinks.

"Did you see what Piper had on this morning?" Tara asked. Her daughter was eight, going on twenty, and insisted on selecting her outfits independently.

"I must have missed her. What was she wearing today?" Maddie chuckled.

"You know... leggings, an old MC Hammer concert tee, mismatched socks, and a TuTu!"

"Like mother, like daughter."

Tara scoffed, amused, "Well, I never..."

"And to think she's in the gifted program..." Maddie joked.

Tara snorted before responding. "They don't judge based on clothing."

"Thank goodness," Maddie laughed.

"So… Why were you honking at Vanessa Sams?" Tara questioned, leaning forward slightly.

A little laugh.

Maddie blinked. "I wasn't honking *at her.* I was having a moment with my steering wheel."

"Semantics." Tara shrugged.

"I didn't know she was going to take it as a personal attack."

Maddie knew Vanessa, but not well. They had been neighbors ever since the Carters moved to Dogwood Bay, and they both had kids in the third grade. From what she could tell, she was nice enough but also particular, always keeping to a structured routine.

Having a child with a disability had its challenges. Maddie often found herself left out of group chats and outings with parents of more typical kids. Maybe because therapy appointments and behaviors dictated her days, or maybe because other parents just didn't understand. Either way.

Tara lowered her voice, despite the fact that no one was paying them any attention.

"She's... intense. Just my opinion." If anyone had opinions, it was Tara.

Maddie snorted.

"No, I mean it," Tara said. "She's always watching.

Always noticing things. Who's late. Who leaves early. Whose car isn't where it should be."

Maddie paused mid-sip. "What? Like, for real?"

Tara nodded. "Donna says that Vanessa is trying to 'help keep the school safe,'" she air quoted. "But honestly? I think it's weird."

"Donna thinks a lot of things," Maddie said. "Almost as much as you." A wink.

"Burn." They both laughed.

Maddie leaned back slightly, processing.

The sunglasses.

The stillness.

The eye contact.

The notebook.

"When it was Piper's turn to bring in treats for class, she actually asked me for the recipe I used... just to make sure I followed the school's allergen-free guidelines." Tara scoffed. "I don't even think Ellie has any allergies!" She paused to take a drink of coffee. "She always puts people in uncomfortable situations, like bringing up things at inappropriate times. Donna told me that just last week, Derek was reported for talking on the phone in the carline... and we all know who reported him."

"Vanessa?"

"Yep. Like, I swear she writes things down. It's the only way she can possibly remember all these things she knows." Tara shook her head.

Maddie fidgeted in her seat and took another sip of her drink. "She does," she said finally.

Tara made eye contact. A collective moment of understanding. She froze. "Wait. What?!"

"I saw her this morning," Maddie said. "She had a notebook. She was writing something. In carline."

Tara's eyes lit up. "I *knew* it!"

"Of course you did."

"It's validating."

Maddie just smiled.

Tara shrugged. "One time, I heard she called the school because someone let their kid out on the wrong side of the car."

Maddie stared at her in disbelief.

"She notices EVERYTHING," Tara was talking so excitedly, she was practically yelling at Maddie now.

"Well, that's not *so* bad. I'm sure Principal Garcia is used to moms like that," Maddie rebutted.

Tara let out a soft laugh. "Probably."

"Oh! I remember that. It was Derek that time, too. He was fuming."

"Retaliating on the group chat." They laughed in unison. "Maybe if he wasn't always on his phone, he could remind his daughter which car door to use."

Maddie glanced down at her phone, then back up. "Still," she said. "I feel like accidentally honking at her just put me on some kind of list."

Tara smirked. "Oh, you're definitely on a list."

CHAPTER 3

MONDAY | CHAOS

BY 3:14 P.M., Maddie was back in the carline.

She tapped her fingers against the steering wheel, watching the slow crawl of cars ahead of her, mentally running through the next few hours like a checklist she already knew she'd struggle to complete. Both mentally and physically.

3:15 p.m. Pickup.
4:00 p.m. OT.
5:30 p.m. Meds.
6:00 p.m. Dinner.
7:30 p.m. Bath.
8:00 p.m. Bed.

Repeat daily until morale improves.

Spoiler: it doesn't.

Sure, Maddie relied on routines. Schedules. Timers. Checklists. The quiet comfort of knowing what came next. But routines in her world weren't guarantees. They were suggestions at best.

Because no matter how well she planned a day, how care-

fully she mapped out transitions and timing, it all came down to one thing she couldn't control: Lennon.

His mood. His tolerance. His capacity for the day.

Some days, everything clicked into place like it was supposed to.

Other days unraveled before breakfast.

And once it started to unravel, there wasn't much she could do except recalibrate and keep moving.

That was the difference between her life and most everyone else's in the carline.

They followed patterns. She adapted to them.

Her phone buzzed in the cupholder again, and she groaned. "No..."

When Lennon made his way to the car, guided by Evan, Maddie felt that familiar mix of relief and nauseating responsibility settle over her.

"Hey, buddy," she said gently as he climbed in, while Evan helped to buckle the seatbelt.

"I want home, please," he said. With his limited speech, Lennon was nothing if not polite. Maddie was starting to hate the word *please,* as Lennon ended almost every request or demand with it these days.

"First OT," she replied, already pulling forward. "Then home."

A pause.

A small shift in the backseat.

"I want home, please," he repeated, louder this time.

Maddie kept her voice even. "First OT, then home."

By the time they pulled into the driveway just after five, Maddie was drained.

At least the car ride home was relaxing... Lennon was consumed by the scenery out the window. Trees, some cows, factories. He flapped his hands, excited about whatever had gotten his attention.

Maddie, Kent, and Lennon had packed up and moved to Dogwood Bay to have a quieter life and to get out of the hustle and bustle of the city. They wanted Lennon to have community. Kent had lived in Dogwood Bay growing up, so he had friends and family here, and Maddie was willing to give it a try. While Dogwood Bay was an hour from anywhere that felt like it mattered, the truth of it was that it was the kind of place people stayed because leaving felt harder than settling.

The front door opened before she even had her keys out.

Joon.

Big. Clumsy. Slightly unhinged.

The dog launched herself forward like a furry missile, nails skidding against the concrete as she circled Maddie and Lennon with frantic energy.

Kent was also halfway out the door.

Running shoes on. The lanyard from his keychain dangling from his pocket. That in-between moment where he wasn't fully gone yet, but also not staying. He had discovered a routine that worked for him in an effort to take better care of himself.

Maddie was proud of him, but also jealous that she didn't have it in her to do the same for herself.

"Hey," he said, pausing just long enough to lean in and kiss her cheek.

"Hey," Maddie replied, shifting her bag higher on her shoulder.

"How was..."

"Don't ask," she said, interrupting, but not unkindly.

He nodded once. "Fair." He glanced at her ever-present frown. "You good?" he asked with a note of concern.

Maddie hesitated just long enough for it to mean something. "Yeah. Just... tired."

He studied her for a second, like he wanted to say more, or ask more, but didn't. "Back in a bit."

"Have a good run," Maddie encouraged.

And then he was gone.

Inside, there was a distinct and immediate absence.

Thunderpaws.

Their cat had made his position on the new living arrangement very clear the moment Joon arrived that January from a rescue group in the city.

He did not approve.

And rather than adapt, he had simply relocated.

Maddie glanced up the stairs.

"Still holding a grudge, huh?" she called, wishing the cat would just get over it so she had one less thing to deal with. "Shoes off," she said automatically, pinging her attention to Lennon before he could escape to the kitchen.

Lennon didn't respond.

Didn't move.

Just stood there, backpack still on, breathing slightly faster and heavier than before.

Maddie softened her tone. "Come on. Shoes. Off."

Slowly, he complied.

Routine mattered.

Even when everything else felt like too much.

"Okay," Maddie said, moving toward the kitchen. "Let's get meds done."

Even their dog required medication. Twice a day. Maddie took the pills and pushed them into the peanut butter-flavored pill pocket, thinking about what a great invention those little things were. She tossed it into Joon's food dish, where she gobbled it up like a treat.

Maddie straightened, grabbing Lennon's pill organizer from the cabinet.

A rainbow of compartments.

Morning. Evening. Bedtime.

Each one filled. And each one necessary.

"Alright, buddy," she said, setting it down.

He approached slowly. Watched. Then took them, one by one, with practiced familiarity. He was so used to it that she met no resistance. Not like she used to.

Maddie swallowed her own medication dry, because she'd forgotten where she'd set her second, and now watered down, drink from U-Brewed.

"Okay," she said, clapping her hands once, more for herself than anyone else. "Dinner."

She reached for the iPad on the counter.

Pressed the button.

Nothing.

She froze. A long sigh escaped.

"Fuck," she said quietly, followed by more profanity-laced thoughts.

Dead. She had forgotten to charge it.

Behind her, Lennon shifted. "I want iPad, please," he said.

Maddie turned slowly. A deep breath... In and out. "Okay," she said carefully. "It just needs to charge..."

"I want iPad, please." Slower this time.

"I know, I just..."

"I want iPad, please." Louder and slower.

The shift was immediate.

Volume. Tension. Panic.

Maddie moved quickly, plugging Lennon's iPad into an outlet and snatching her own from her bag. She hated giving it up to him on nights like these. A constant fear that it would be thrown or spilled on, but it was the only choice when the other option was Lennon's lack of understanding, rage, and ultimately a meltdown.

The solution had to be immediate.

Lennon's breathing changed back to normal.

Maddie closed her eyes for half a second. "Okay," she whispered. "Okay, we're okay."

A breath.

She wasn't sure who she was trying to convince.

Dinner happened anyway.

Through the noise. Through the pacing. Through the kind of overstimulation that both she and Lennon were experiencing in two vastly different ways.

She moved on autopilot.

The front door opened at 6:30.

Kent.

Right on time.

He stepped inside, slightly out of breath, already reaching for the hem of his shirt to toss it into the hamper. "Hey..."

"Hey," Maddie said, not turning. "Time?"

"11-minute miles, getting better." He took in the scene quickly.

The noise. The tension.

"Rough one?"

She let out a short laugh. "When isn't it?"

He nodded. If anyone understood, it was Kent. "Gonna shower," he said. "Then I'll take over." He would watch over Lennon for the remaining hour, or maybe just minutes, until bathtime. Giving Madison a much-needed break and enough time to pretend that the constant suggestions of self-care made an ounce of difference.

"Yep."

And just like that, he disappeared up the stairs.

Kent was the opposite of Maddie in many ways. She was obsessive, he was nonchalant. She was quiet; he could talk your ear off. She was curious, and he didn't have a perceptive bone in his body. He was a good man, and despite their differences, it worked.

By the time bedtime came, Maddie felt hollowed out. She lay beside Lennon in his room, staring at the ceiling, his breathing deep and loud.

The monitor, ready for business. The locks on the doors, ready to be armed.

Precautions.

Because once, just once, he'd made it out the front door.

And they hadn't known.

Not until the knock.

A neighbor found him.

Ring camera alerted them, they said.

Thank goodness.

Maddie squeezed her eyes shut at the memory.

Never again.

With Lennon finally asleep, she pressed a soft kiss to his forehead. "Night, buddy," she whispered. "Love you."

She slipped out of the room quietly, checking to make sure the monitor was connected to her phone, double-checking the locks on Lennon's door, followed by the garage, the back slider, and the front. She escorted Joon to her crate and cleaned the litter box before washing her hands and face and heading to her and Kent's bedroom.

She didn't bother changing.

Didn't bother with anything, really.

She sat on the edge of the bed.

Then leaned back.

Just for a second.

She was asleep before her head fully hit the pillow.

CHAPTER 4

TUESDAY | MISSING

MADISON PULLED into the school at 8:28 a.m.

She sat in the carline, engine idling, hands resting lightly on the steering wheel. The school doors were still closed, the usual morning chaos not quite in full swing yet. It gave everything a strange, quiet-before-the-storm feeling she wasn't fond of.

From the backseat, Lennon hummed loudly; his migraine-inducing verbal stims were starting to increase in intensity. His fingers tapped against the window in a steady rhythm that usually meant he was regulating. Or thinking. Or both.

Maddie glanced at him in the rearview mirror, then back toward the carline.

She told herself she wasn't looking for anything in particular. Or anyone. Not even her. ***Vanessa.***

But her eyes moved anyway. From car to car, windshield to windshield, searching without fully committing.

The oversized sunglasses.
The too-perfect posture.
The notebook.

Nothing.

Maddie exhaled slowly and leaned back against her seat.

"Okay," she muttered under her breath. "Maybe she's just not here yet."

Which should have been a relief.

It almost was.

Except now that she'd noticed the absence, she couldn't quite un-notice it.

"We wait," she said aloud, more for herself than for Lennon.

"I want wait, please," he echoed from the backseat.

She smiled faintly.

The line began to fill in around them, familiar in that way that routines always were. Donna's SUV rolled in, already mid-conversation with someone through her open window before she'd even fully stopped.

Ryan pulled in behind Maddie, tapping his steering wheel to the beat of the music Maddie could hear through his window.

Ryan Patel, dad to AJ and Michael, member of the third-grade group chat.

The bus line gathered its usual collection of oversized backpacks and barely contained energy.

Everything looked exactly the same.

And yet… Maddie found herself scanning again.

Still, no Vanessa.

She shifted slightly in her seat, a small, restless movement she didn't quite register.

"She's not here," Maddie said quietly, before she could stop herself.

A light knock on her partially rolled-down window made her jump.

Tara stood there, eyebrows raised, clearly amused. "Who's

not here?" she asked abruptly as Maddie unlocked the door, and she slid into the passenger seat like it was her assigned spot.

Maddie hesitated, then gave a small shrug. "Vanessa."

Tara glanced toward the front of the line, scanning quickly.

"Huh," she said. "You're right."

"Probably nothing," Maddie added.

"Probably," Tara agreed easily, already reaching for her phone to see the time. "Still early."

But Maddie noticed it, the way she looked again. Just once more.

Throughout the school year, Vanessa had never missed drop-off. Or even been late.

This wasn't nothing.

It *was* something.

By the time Miss Merissa appeared and began greeting students, the moment had mostly passed, and Lennon had lost his composure. Waiting was not his strong suit, and Maddie had missed the sweet spot between arriving too early and too late. He was flailing about, demanding home. Head knocking into the headrest behind him, feet kicking the passenger seat in front of him. This time, without the "please."

The pickup line had to veer left to get around Madison's car for the ten minutes it took her to calm Lennon.

Once he did, Maddie helped him unbuckle, handing over his backpack and lunch to Evan.

"Have a good day, my little love," sadness was behind Maddie's voice.

With Evan's help, he stepped out of the car with his usual pause before joining his class.

Crisis averted. Mostly.

Routine intact. Sort of.

Another small win.

Maddie watched him go, letting out a breath she didn't realize she'd been holding. When she looked up again, her eyes instinctively flicked throughout the lot.

Still, no Vanessa. And the "it being early" excuse no longer flew.

But it wasn't her business.

It wasn't anything.

Just a missing car.

Just a parent who didn't show up.

Kids were absent from school all the time.

It wasn't until later that morning, standing in her kitchen with her laptop open and her first energy drink of the day sitting untouched beside her, that she noticed texts were coming through.

3rd Grade Group Chat – MUTED

She stared at it for a second before giving in and tapping it open.

She rarely checked the thread. It was mostly irrelevant and unnecessary noise. Fundraiser reminders, spirit days, and way too many exclamation points.

But today was different.

Donna
Has anyone seen Vanessa Sams?

Maddie's attention perked.

She scrolled.

Donna
Vanessa didn't do drop-off and Ellie wasn't at school today 😩

Parent #1
Weird... doesn't Ellie have perfect attendance?

One of these days, Maddie would put a name to the unknown numbers on this chat. All she knew was that they were parents of third graders.

Donna
Perfect attendance for 4 years!!!

Tara
🙃 Like going to school sick is something to be proud of.

Chloe
Oh yeah, and she was supposed to bring snacks for the class today too.

Parent #2
I forgot about that... my kids said they were excited for cupcakes today!

Kids? Who has more than one? That must be Ryan or Anika; they have twins.

Donna
Exactly🎯 Vanessa does not miss things like that.

Maddie shifted her weight, rereading that line. "Does not miss things like that," she said to herself.

Mark
Maybe they're just sick?

Donna
Maybe. I texted her this morning and haven't heard back yet.

Chloe
That's not like her!!!

Lindsay
Derek wasn't there with Sara either. Maybe there's a bug going around.

Parent #1
That's probably it.

Mark
Probably.

The messages kept coming, but slower now. Less chatter. Eventually, the chat went silent, and the parents moved on to more important things.

But by the time pick-up rolled around that afternoon...

She was looking for Vanessa again.

And her notebook.

CHAPTER 5
WEDNESDAY | UNEASY

BY THE SECOND MORNING, it stopped feeling like a coincidence.

Maddie pulled into the carline at 8:35. Not early this time, not late.

She was focused on getting in and getting out. She had work to do. No time for conversations or distractions.

Except that the second her tires rolled into the lot, she noticed.

She felt it immediately this time. That small, quiet tightening in her chest that didn't quite qualify as worry, but definitely wasn't nothing either.

"Okay," she muttered, more firmly than yesterday. "Still normal."

From the backseat, Lennon echoed loudly, "I want normal, please."

Maddie huffed out a short laugh. "Exactly. You and me both, buddy."

The line crept forward in slow, familiar increments. Donna was mid-conversation with someone two cars ahead.

Tara's car slid in a few spaces behind Maddie, close

enough that she could see her gesturing animatedly as she talked, even from a distance.

Everything else looked exactly the same.

Which somehow made the two missing pieces stand out even more.

Vanessa wasn't there.

Derek wasn't there.

By the time Lennon made his way out of the car, guided by Miss Merissa's steady, practiced calm, Maddie had already checked the carline at least six times.

Not that she was counting.

"Have a good day, buddy," she said, smoothing his hair as he stepped out.

"I want good day, please," he replied.

"You got it," she replied in a motherly calm.

She watched him walk away, pause, then continue forward. Routine holding.

Tara and Maddie once again met up at U-Brewed for caffeine and gossip.

"Did you see the group chat?" Tara asked.

Maddie sighed. "I did. Against my better judgment."

"Same."

A pause.

"You think they're sick?" Tara asked.

"I mean... probably," Maddie said. "I probably wouldn't have even noticed Derek being gone if someone didn't mention it."

"Same," Tara agreed. "Vanessa, on the other hand..."

Neither of them sounded convinced.

. . .

It wasn't until Maddie was back home, standing in her kitchen with her laptop open and her energy drink sweating onto the counter, that the group chat started flowing again.

This time, she didn't hesitate.

3rd Grade Group Chat – MUTED

Donna
Okay, has anyone actually heard from Vanessa?

Thirty seconds. No response.

Donna
According to my sources, Ellie's absences aren't excused. That's not like our Vanessa.

Maddie leaned against the counter, reading.

Lindsay
So Vanessa didn't even call her out? 😬

Tara
Maybe she doesn't know how. 🤣 I mean, it would be the first time.

The parents all started to chime in, one after another, that no, they had in fact not heard from Vanessa.

Donna
I tried calling this morning. Straight to voicemail.

That made Maddie pause.

Chloe
That's... weird. Just tried. Voicemail for me too.

Lindsay
Maybe they went out of town? ✈️

Donna
Without telling anyone? And missing school? An unexcused absence? That doesn't sound like Vanessa.

There it was again.

That phrase.

Doesn't sound like Vanessa.

She set her phone down.

Picked it back up.

Set it down again.

Her teeth bit her bottom lip like she was considering something uncharacteristically friendly, something a more active participant in the group chat would do.

After all, she had work to do.

Emails to answer.

Laundry that had been sitting in the dryer since yesterday. And, let's be real, probably some in the washing machine too.

She had a dog that needed attention.

A child with a full afternoon schedule.

A house in complete disarray.

She did not need to insert herself into whatever *this* was.

Her phone buzzed.

Tara
Okay but like... what if something actually happened?

Maddie stared at the message.

Typed.

Deleted.

Typed again.

Maddie
I did see her SUV in her driveway.

Tara
They've got to be home then. People don't just disappear.

Maddie
Exactly.

She pushed herself off the counter and walked to the sink, staring out the window down the quiet street leading to Vanessa's house. You had to pass it to get to Maddie's, which sat at the end of the cul-de-sac.

Out the window, the street looked like it always did.

Same houses.

Same parked cars.

Same everything.

Until now. Something was off, but Maddie wasn't seeing it yet.

"This is a terrible idea," she said out loud as she shook her head.

Joon looked up from where she was sprawled on the floor, tail thumping repeatedly in what Maddie decided was agreement.

She grabbed her phone.

Opened the group chat.

And before she could think better of it...

Maddie
They live on my street. I can swing by later and check on them.

Hesitation. Finger hovering over send.

She closed her eyes as if willing herself not to get involved.

Send.

A groan escaped.

"Why would you do that?" she whispered to herself.

Her phone buzzed almost instantly.

Donna
That would be amazing, Madison!!!

Of course it would.

Chloe
Thank you so much!!!

Mark
I'm telling you, you're worried for nothing.

Lindsay
Better to check, just to make sure everything's okay.

Tara
Report back 👀

Maddie let her head fall back slightly. Eyes closed, she rubbed her temples.

What did she just do?

Volunteering for something she didn't have to do? That wasn't like her.

Plus, Mark lives *right next door* to Vanessa. Why hadn't he stepped up? Donna, too. She lived just a few blocks over. Oh well, it was done. She said she'd do it, and she would.

Three hours later, after a full afternoon of responsibilities, Maddie stood in her kitchen, staring out the window toward Vanessa's house.

A perfect house with a perfect lawn. Flowers lined the front walkway, and two Dogwood trees bloomed in shades of pink. And while she couldn't see the backyard, she assumed it was just as impeccable.

She didn't know the Sams' family schedule, what cars should be there, or when. She didn't know if they had pets or what time they went to bed.

Was Vanessa married? No? Maybe? Maddie vaguely remembered that she was a single mom like Tara. But she wasn't sure.

All she really knew was that Vanessa had a daughter, Ellie, in the third grade, and that Vanessa drove a white SUV.

Maybe if Ellie ever invited Lennon to play with her or if they were in the same classroom, she'd know more. But no. Other third graders didn't typically invite Lennon over for play dates. Lennon was in a separate classroom, one reserved for students like him. It wasn't until Tara added her to the group chat that the other parents even knew she existed and had a child in the third grade. One that they had rarely seen outside of the carline.

Joon lifted her head from the floor, ears perked, like she'd been personally invited into the decision-making process.

Maddie looked down at her. "This is a terrible idea," she groaned. "You want to be my bodyguard?"

Joon's tail thumped repeatedly and excitedly against the tile.

"Let's go." Maddie motioned toward the door with a tilt of her head.

The evening air was starting to cool down; they had the kind of humid heat that settled in early and didn't leave except for a rare breeze after dark. Maddie slipped her phone into her pocket and started down the sidewalk, Joon trotting beside her like this was the most exciting thing that had ever happened.

"Don't get any ideas," Maddie told her. "You're here for moral support."

Joon glanced up at her, tongue lolling.

Moral support. Zero actual protection.

Big dog. Intimidating, technically.

Still... Maddie felt better having her.

The cul-de-sac was quiet.

Too quiet? Maybe.

Or maybe Maddie was just paying more attention than usual.

A sprinkler clicked somewhere in the distance. A garage door hummed closed. Otherwise, nothing.

Everything looked normal.

Maddie waved at Greg, the sole member of the neighborhood watch. He was sitting on his front porch, observing the neighborhood. He returned the gesture with a gentle smile and a wave.

Vanessa's house looked the same as always. At least as far as Maddie remembered it.

It was neat. Put together. The kind of house that looked like it followed rules that didn't even exist within their HOA.

Maddie slowed her steps.

Her eyes went immediately to the driveway.

There was Vanessa's SUV.

Maddie stepped onto the path leading up to the front door.

The perfect path, lined with perfect flowers.

"Just a quick check," she said, more to herself than the dog.

She walked up to the front door and pressed the button on the video doorbell. She heard the tune play from inside the house.

Waited.

Nothing.

She shifted her weight, listening.

No movement inside. No footsteps. No muffled sound of a TV or voices. No dog barking.

Just... quiet.

"Hello. It's your neighbor," Maddie said into the camera. "Madison." Just in case someone was watching.

She rang again, followed by a knock, for good measure.

Still nothing.

Joon wandered a few steps to the side, nose already working overtime as she sniffed along the edge of the house. A trained bloodhound, she was not. Probably looking for food.

"Don't be weird," Maddie scolded, glancing back once toward the street. Greg was eying her with curiosity and maybe a little suspicion.

Nothing actually looked out of place.

"Alright," she said, turning slightly. "We're leaving. We did our good deed. That's enough."

She took a step back down the walkway.

Then paused.

Something felt... off.

Not obvious.

Not dramatic.

Just... wrong.

Her eyes drifted toward the side of the house. To the gate. The gate was steel. Standard. The kind you barely noticed. The kind that protected everyone who lived on the street's backyard.

Maddie noticed that it wasn't fully closed.

Just slightly open.

She hesitated for half a second.

The kind of half-second where a smarter or less curious person might turn around.

She didn't.

Just a quick peek, she told herself.

CHAPTER 6
WEDNESDAY | WRONG

THE GATE CREAKED SLIGHTLY as Maddie pushed it open.

Not loud.

But loud enough that Maddie worried someone would see her and think she was up to something.

She winced, instinctively glancing back toward the street like someone might be watching. Greg appeared to have moved inside.

"This is fine," she muttered. "This isn't illegal. We're just... checking. We're being good citizens."

Joon slipped through the opening ahead of her, tail wagging like they'd just arrived at a park instead of performing some trespassing-adjacent behavior.

"Great," Maddie whispered. "Lead the way. No pressure."

The backyard was exactly as she expected.

Not messy.

Not chaotic.

It was clean, controlled.

A bit too controlled.

The lawn had recently been mowed, as Maddie could smell the grass in the air around her. Patio furniture arranged as if for a *Better Homes and Gardens* spread. A small outdoor table sat off to the side, untouched, like it had been staged for entertaining guests, but they had yet to break it in.

Maddie stepped forward slowly, her sneakers crunching lightly against a gravel pathway leading to the porch.

"Hello?" she called, her voice automatically dropping lower.

Nothing.

No answer.

No movement.

Joon's pace slowed.

Not dramatically.

Just enough.

Her tail still wagged, but not as wildly now, her nose moving in shorter, more focused bursts.

Maddie noticed.

"Don't start being competent now," she murmured.

Something shifted in the air.

It wasn't a smell, not exactly.

Not strong enough to name.

Just... off.

Maddie took another step forward.

Then another.

Her eyes moved across the yard, trying to take in details she wouldn't normally notice. The hair on her arms stood on end.

Everything normal, and everything wrong.

Joon stopped.

Completely.

That, more than anything, made Maddie's stomach drop.
"Joon?" she said quietly.
The dog didn't move.
Just stood there, staring toward the far edge of the patio.
Maddie followed her line of sight.
At first, she didn't understand what she was looking at.
Her brain tried to make it something else.

A pile of something?
A shadow?
A trick of the light?

Then... It clicked.

The shape.
The stillness.
The way it definitely didn't belong.
And most definitely not in Vanessa's yard.

Maddie's breath caught in her throat. "Oh, my God."
She didn't move closer. Couldn't.
Because now that she saw it, she *really* saw it. And there was no unseeing it.

A body.

Maddie stumbled back a step, one hand flying up to cover her mouth.
"No, no, no, no…" she sputtered.
Joon let out a low, uncertain sound, pacing, unsure what this situation required of her.
And honestly?
Same.
Maddie's heart slammed against her ribs, loud enough that she was sure it had to be audible.

"This is not happening," she whispered.

But it was. It very much was.

Her eyes darted around the yard again, suddenly hyper-aware.

"They're not home," she said, the realization landing all at once.

"They're not home, and there's a..." She couldn't finish the sentence.

Her hands shook as she fumbled for her phone.

Dropped it. Swore. Picked it up again.

9-1-1

Her thumb hovered for half a second.

The same kind of half-second that had gotten her here in the first place.

Then she hit call.

Her next thought was: What was she going to tell the group chat?

CHAPTER 7
WEDNESDAY | SIRENS

MADDIE DIDN'T REMEMBER ENDING the call.

One second, she was talking, words tumbling out too fast, not fast enough, and the next she was standing in the middle of the backyard, phone still in her hand, heart pounding so very hard.

Joon pressed against her leg, unusually still now, as if she finally understood the depth; this wasn't a game.

"It's okay," Maddie whispered, though nothing about this was okay.

She backed toward the gate, eyes locked on the body even as every instinct told her to look away.

She didn't.

Couldn't.

The sirens came faster than she expected.

Distant at first. Then closer. Then *everywhere.*

Maddie stepped out onto the sidewalk just as the first patrol car turned onto the street, lights flashing against the quiet, ordinary houses. Very out of place.

Everything about this was.

The officer who approached her was calm. Like this was

just another Wednesday. "Ma'am, are you the one who called?"

Maddie nodded, her voice catching slightly. "Yeah. I... yes. I found... I found him."

"Okay," he said gently. After introducing himself as Officer Jones, "I'm going to need you to step back over here for me."

A buzz from her phone as she waited for further instructions.

Kent
Where are you?

Maddie
At Vanessa's. Look outside.

Kent
What's going on? U okay?

Maddie
Yeah, Joon is with me. Talk when I get home.

Kent
OK. Be safe. Love you.

Maddie was about to lose her composure, but she knew she couldn't ask Kent to come. He was with Lennon, and Lennon needed him. That was more important right now. Lennon had to come first.

By the time they taped off the yard, Maddie was sitting on the curb with a bottle of water she didn't remember being handed.

Joon lay across her feet, finally calm, like she'd decided her job was to stay.

"Is that your dog?" the officer asked.

Maddie nodded. "Yeah. She's... not helpful."

Joon's tongue once again lolling out the side of her mouth.

The officer's mouth twitched slightly into a grin. "She's doing alright. Can you walk me through what happened?" He pulled out a small notebook.

Maddie blinked at it.

A notebook.

Her stomach turned. She shook her head before collecting herself.

She noticed neighbors gathering, congregating at a makeshift barricade. First Greg, then Mark, a few other familiar and unknown faces.

"Uh... yeah," she said. "I... I live down the street. We noticed they weren't at school yesterday. Or today. And someone mentioned it in a text, and I just... I said I'd check on them."

She winced slightly at how that sounded out loud.

"Okay," he said, writing. "And you came over alone?"

Maddie glanced down at Joon. "I had my backup."

That earned a small huff of a laugh.

"Walk me through it," the officer directed.

"I knocked. Rang the doorbell. No answer. I was leaving, but then I saw the back gate open."

"You entered the backyard?"

A second passed.

"…Yes." A gulp. Was she in trouble?

"Alright."

No judgment. Just writing.

"And that's when you saw the body?"

Maddie nodded, swallowing hard. "Yeah."

"Did you touch anything?"

"No."

"See anyone else?"

"No."

"Any vehicles in the driveway?"

"Just Vanessa's SUV."

The officer nodded, jotting everything down.

Another officer approached, speaking quietly to him.

Maddie caught fragments.

"… adult male..."

"… time of death unclear..."

"… no one else inside..."

Her stomach plummeted. "Was that a good thing? No one else inside?" she thought to herself. "If there was no one inside, where were Vanessa and Ellie?"

The officer hesitated, then gave a careful nod. "We're not seeing signs of anyone else at the moment. Just the deceased."

Maddie's mind raced.

Vanessa.

Ellie.

Gone.

"Do you know the family that lives here?" he asked.

"A little," Maddie admitted. "Just... school. Carline. Our kids are both in third grade."

"Names?"

"Vanessa Sams. Her daughter, Ellie. Where are they?"

The officer exchanged a glance with the other one.

That look.

The one that said something without saying it.

Ignoring her question, he asked another. "Did you know the deceased?"

"I... no... I couldn't look," Maddie whispered her response.

"That's alright, ma'am. I understand how difficult this is."

A moment passed.

"Alright," he said, straightening slightly. "We'll be in touch so you can make your official statement tomorrow."

. . .

The sirens faded into background noise, and neighbors continued to gather at the edges of the street... Whispering, watching, speculating.

Police circulated - each playing what Maddie assumed was a vital role in gaining an understanding of what had happened here.

Madison retreated home, head down, Joon walking casually at her side. But one thing settled heavily in her chest.

Vanessa wasn't the kind of person who missed things.

Not school.
Not responsibilities.
Not control.

And now she was gone.
With a body in her backyard.

CHAPTER 8
THURSDAY | NOISE

AFTER DROPPING Lennon off at school and escaping carline unharmed, Madison headed to the police station to give her official statement.

The police station felt colder than it should have.

Not temperature cold. Just... sterile. Quiet in a way that made every sound feel louder than it was. Everything here seemed to have an echo.

Maddie sat in the chair across from Officer Jones, her hands folded tightly in her lap, then unfolding, then folding again.

He had a notebook open. Not a green one.

A different one.

Official.

"Just walk me through your morning," he said. "Start from when you got to the school."

Maddie nodded, swallowing.

"Okay. Um... I got there around 8:30. Maybe a little after. The carline was already long, which isn't unusual." She heard her own voice and thought it sounded strange. Too calm. Too organized for how her brain actually felt. "I saw that Vanessa wasn't there. She's usually there. Always, actually."

"Always?" he asked.

Maddie nodded. "Yeah. At the same time. Every day."

He scribbled something down.

"Ellie had perfect attendance," she continued.

Patterns.

Of course.

"I didn't think anything of it at first," Maddie continued. "Kids get sick. Things happen. But then... someone said she hadn't responded to texts. And that Ellie's absences were unexcused."

"And that concerned you?"

Maddie hesitated. "It wasn't just that. It was... her. She's consistent."

Officer Jones looked up briefly. "Consistent how?"

"Routine. She followed one. Very closely."

He nodded slightly, like that meant something to him. "Okay. What happened next?"

Maddie walked him through it. The texts. The decision to check. The walk over.

Her voice tightened when she got to the part about the backyard.

"I didn't go looking for anything," she said quickly. "I just... I noticed the gate was open."

"And then you saw the body."

She nodded.

Silence settled for a moment.

"Did you recognize him?" he asked.

"No," Maddie said immediately. "Not then."

"His name is Derek. Derek Holloway. Are you familiar?"

"Carline," Maddie whispered, in shock from what she had just been told. "His daughter is Sara..." She trailed off.

His name felt heavy.

He jotted something else down, closed the notebook, and had her sign her official statement.

"That's all I need for now," he said, standing. "I'm going

to step out for a minute. Someone will be by in a moment to walk you out."

Maddie nodded. "Okay."

He paused at the door. "And Mrs. Carter?"

She looked up.

"Try not to talk too much about this with other parents. Things can get... messy."

Maddie gave a small, tight smile. "Okay, I'll try."

The door clicked shut behind him.

The room went still.

Maddie exhaled slowly, her shoulders dropping just slightly.

Her eyes drifted.

Not intentionally.

Just something to focus on.

A desk sat off to the side, papers stacked unevenly. A laptop sat open, screen dimmed but not off.

She told herself not to look.

She looked anyway.

Just a glance.

Maddie shifted slightly in her chair, leaning just enough to catch the screen at an angle.

A photo.

Her stomach dropped.

It was the backyard.

Vanessa's backyard.

She recognized the patio. The furniture. The angle.

And then, Derek.

He was lying on his side near the edge of the patio.

Too still. Too wrong.

There was blood near his head. Not everywhere. Just

enough.

Maddie leaned a little farther without thinking, her chair tilting slightly beneath her.

A line of text sat beneath the image.

She squinted.

"Blunt force trauma..."

Her chair leg slipped. Maddie jerked back, grabbing the edge of the table to steady herself.

"Oh my God," she sputtered, two officers eyeing her with a knowing look.

She sat upright immediately, staring straight ahead.

Blunt force.

Not planned.

Not distant.

Close.

Fast.

About an hour after arriving, she left the station and officially unmuted the group chat.

The entire drive home was a chorus of buzzing.

Maybe she should mute it again...

Maddie arrived home, laptop sitting on the counter in front of her, poised to do her actual job and not speculate about the whys and whos of this investigation. With each buzz, her phone rattled against the granite like it had something urgent to say.

Which, unfortunately, it probably did.

She stared at it for a full five seconds before giving in.

Mistake. Now she was absolutely going to fall behind on work.

3rd Grade Group Chat

Donna
Okay, I'm just going to say it because clearly no one else is...

A moment.

Donna
It was Derek Holloway.

How'd she find out so fast?

Lindsay
WAIT!!! 😮 Like, actually Derek?? Sara's dad Derek??

Donna
Yes. That Derek.

Chloe
My god.

Lindsay
I literally just saw him!!!

Donna
Exactly. This is what I'm saying.

Parent #1
Do we know what happened??

Donna
Not officially.

Lindsay
I heard it was at Vanessa's house...

Tara
It was. Maddie found his body.

Maddie's grip tightened slightly on her phone.

There it was.

No longer a rumor.

No longer a question.

But it was begging a question. Does she respond? Was that her place? Would the police care? Certainly, it was better than having the third grade parent rumor mill take control of the narrative.

Parent #2
Was he murdered?

Lindsay
Probably, I don't think he was winning any personality contests.

Chloe
This is crazy. We're supposed to be a safe town.

Tara
And now we have murderers as neighbors!

Mark
Let's not jump to conclusions.

Maddie paused at that one.

He was short.

Controlled.

Different.

And they were all jumping to conclusions.

Lindsay
I mean... I'm not saying anything, but I always thought something was off with him.

Donna
Off how??

Lindsay
Just... secretive? Idk. Hard to explain. Like he was up to no good.

Maddie frowned.

That didn't help.

If anything, it made everything feel worse.

Chloe
What does this have to do with Vanessa?? Where is she?

The chat slowed.

A rare pause.

Then...

Donna
She's not answering anyone. And neither is Ellie.

Silence again.

Heavier this time.

Lindsay
Okay, but like... where are they??

Parent #2
I'm sure they've spoken to the police.

Donna
No, I heard they can't find them.

Word travels fast in Dogwood Bay.

Parent #1
Do you think they're involved???

Lindsay
Obv. It was at her house!!!

Mark
You're speculating.

Donna
But it absolutely means something.

Maddie locked her phone and set it face down on the counter.

She had to step away. "Not my problem."

From the living room, Joon barked once.

Maddie nodded. "Correct."

Her phone buzzed again.

Tara
Tell me everything. 😳

Maddie typed before she could overthink it.

Maddie
I'm not speaking to you! You outed me on there.

Tara
🙁 I had to say something!

Maddie
Not that!

A moment passed.

Maddie
It was horrible.

Tara
I'm coming over.

Twenty minutes later, Tara stood in her kitchen, U-Brewed drinks in hand, lilac sunglasses covering her tired eyes. Clearly, Tara hadn't fully committed to being awake yet.

"You found Derek, huh?" she said.

Maddie nodded. "Yeah."

Tara blinked. "Like... *our* Derek?"

"Unless there's another Derek Holloway walking around that I missed."

"Okay, but that's..." Tara stopped. Processing everything. "That's worse."

"Yep."

They stood there for a moment, the weight of it all settling in.

Then Tara leaned forward slightly. "You know him, right?"

Maddie nodded slowly. "Yeah. Not like *know* him. I don't know everyone like you do. But I've seen him. Carline. Around."

"He didn't seem like..." Tara trailed off.

"Like someone who ends up dead in someone else's backyard?" Maddie offered.

"Exactly."

A pause.

"And Vanessa?" Tara asked.

Maddie shook her head. "That part makes even less sense."

Her phone buzzed again.

Maddie ignored it this time.

Because for the first time since yesterday, she wasn't just reacting.

She was thinking.

And something about this clearly didn't fit.

CHAPTER 9
THURSDAY | QUESTIONS

CARLINE FELT DIFFERENT.

Not visibly.

Not in any way you could point to.

People weren't acting strangely. They were still going through the motions.

But Maddie felt a shift the second she pulled in.

The usual tempo had altered itself. It was quieter, tighter, like conversations were happening in smaller spaces, just out of reach. Heads leaned in closer. Voices dropped to lower decibels. People looked up more often than they should. Yet at the same time, they were looking down, trying to go unnoticed, as insignificant bystanders to a crime.

Donna was still talking, of course she was, but even she seemed slightly more controlled, her voice lowered just enough to suggest she understood the weight of what she was saying. No longer flippant and nonchalant, now serious and more calculated.

Maddie assumed she was gathering information. The details were need-to-know, and Donna *needed to know*.

Tara slid into the spot behind Maddie, catching her eye

through the windshield with a look that said, "We are absolutely talking about this."

Maddie gave a small nod.

Of course they were.

As the carline crept forward, Maddie found herself watching people instead of just glancing over them.

Lindsay stood near the sidewalk. She walked her son Toby to school every day. She was mid-conversation, her hands moving as she talked, animated, invested, like she had something to contribute to every version of the story.

Lindsay Smith, mom to Toby, member of the third-grade group chat

Mark lingered a few feet away, arms crossed, posture closed off. He had parked to help his daughter, Juniper, carry in what looked to be a tray of cookies. He wasn't talking much. When he did, people leaned in. He spoke with a no-nonsense type of authority. When Mark spoke, people listened.

Mark Sweeney, dad to Juniper, member of the third-grade group chat

Mark had once been a big-city cop and was from St. Louis, like the Carters. Maddie had pieced together that the move to Dogwood Bay had come about eight years ago, after they had Juniper, and his wife wanted to be closer to her parents. So now, instead of patrols and paperwork, he spends his mornings in the carline and his evenings working at their family business. Together, he and his wife, Sonja, ran a flower shop, The Pretty Petal.

Maddie couldn't help but wonder how that shift sat with him. How would a year of small-town routines feel for someone who used to live in constant motion?

Chloe sat in her car, windows rolled up. Definitely

observing more than the rest, quieter than the rest. Her attention moved between conversations without fully joining any of them. Maddie knew Chloe and Vanessa had been tight, but with Maddie, Chloe always seemed a little guarded. Did she know something?

Chloe Keene, mom to Keaton, member of the third-grade group chat.

Chloe also seemed panicked on the group text. Like extremely worried.

Tara parked and ran over to Maddie's car after Piper got out and ran up to her teacher.

"You look like you're profiling people," Tara said in a sing-song fashion, sliding into the passenger seat.

"I'm not profiling," Maddie said.

"You're absolutely profiling," Tara said matter-of-factly. "No judgment."

"I'm observing."

"Same thing." A wink.

Maddie glanced toward Lindsay, nudging her head in that direction so Tara's eyes would follow. "She said Derek was 'off.'"

Tara followed her gaze. "Yeah. I tracked that."

"A little convenient, don't you think?" Maddie questioned.

"What do you mean?"

"I think she likes being right. Now, when there is some justification, she can say she knew it all along."

Tara smirked. "She's Donna Junior."

They chuckled.

Maddie retorted, "Exactly. Donna knows everything, and Lindsay wants to pretend she does."

Another laugh.

"And Mark," Tara added, lowering her voice slightly. "Did you see that message?"

"'Don't speculate?" Maddie said.

"Yeah."

Maddie frowned. "That stood out."

"Right? Everyone else is spiraling, and he's just... calm."

Maddie's eyes drifted toward him again.

He was talking now. At least on the group chat.

Maddie noted that he had rarely chimed in on the group text before, but now he was.

"Maybe he just doesn't like group chats," Tara suggested. "Or that since this was once his field of expertise, now he has to reign us all in to minimize gossip."

"Or," Maddie countered, "maybe he knows something."

That sat between them.

Not heavy. Not yet.

But noticeable.

Maddie exhaled slowly, glancing back toward the front of the carline. "I hate this."

Tara nodded. "Same."

Because now... this wasn't just something that happened. It was something that involved people they knew.

Maddie looked from person to person, trying to note any changes in behavior. Was anyone absent other than the obvious? Was anyone avoiding eye contact when they spoke?

These were the people they saw every day. People they were now looking at just a little differently.

CHAPTER 10
THURSDAY | PATTERNS

BY EVENING, Maddie had officially done zero work.

Her laptop sat open in front of her, the same email half-written for the last forty-five minutes. The cursor was blinking aggressively at her, expecting the effort that she usually gave daily. It expected her to do what she did on every childless morning, energy drink in the other hand.

Instead, she stared at her phone.

At the group chat.

At the names.

1. Tara. *Mom to Piper.*
2. Donna. *Mom to Laura.*
3. Lindsay. *Mom to Toby.*
4. Mark. *Dad to Juniper.*
5. Chloe. *Mom to Keaton.*
6. Derek. (now deceased) *Dad to Sara.*
7. Vanessa. (now missing) *Mom to Ellie.* (also missing)

That just left a few unknown numbers. There were AJ & Michael's (twins) parents, Ryan & Anika, and one of the

numbers was certainly theirs. Plus Allison's, Jackson's, and David's (all bus riders) parents.

People she didn't know. Not really.
People she *sort of* knew.
People she now couldn't stop thinking about.

Derek had known all of them.

Or at least...
He had been part of it.
Part of the same routine.
The same ecosystem.

And Vanessa had been watching all of it.

Maddie sat up slightly. The thought landed differently this time.

Not as a joke or as gossip, but as something real.

"She wasn't just being nosy," Maddie murmured. "It was more than that. It was like she was tracking something. But what?"

Joon lifted her head from the floor, immediately alert to the shift in tone.

"And why?"

A tilt of the head from Joon, perhaps she too, was intrigued by this line of thought.

"I mean... she literally wrote things down," Maddie continued.

Her eyes drifted toward her phone again.

Toward the group chat.

Toward the constant stream of information.

Information Vanessa would have had.

Maddie's stomach tightened.

"What if..." she started, then stopped.

Joon's tail thumped once.

Encouraging her, apparently.

"What if she noticed something?"

A pause.

"Something she shouldn't have."

The room felt quieter.

Heavier.

Maddie stood abruptly, pacing once across the kitchen.

"Okay, no. That's... no."

But it didn't feel like a no.

It felt like the beginning of something.

And Maddie was spiraling.

Her phone rang.

It was Tara.

"Hey. I was just about to call you," Maddie said. "You're thinking about it, aren't you?"

Tara exhaled. "Yeah."

"Same," Maddie replied.

A pause.

"We should talk to people," Maddie suggested. She stopped pacing, waiting for confirmation.

"Talk to people?" Tara repeated. "We are not the police."

"Casually," Maddie added. "Not weird."

"I am absolutely going to be weird," Tara said, giving a curtsy to herself. "And you will definitely be awkward, it's part of your charm."

"And what about her notebook?"

"What about it?"

"It might have a clue," Maddie was in full-fledged detective mode now.

"Then I guess we'll need it too," Tara unapologetically agreed.

Maddie glanced out the window toward the street.

The same houses, same driveways, and the same routines.

Only now... She wasn't just part of it; she was paying attention.

"Okay," she said finally.

"Okay," Tara echoed.

And just like that...

They had a plan.

CHAPTER 11
FRIDAY | ASKING

MADDIE IMMEDIATELY REGRETTED THE PLAN.

Not the idea of it.

Just... actually doing it.

Carline was, in hindsight, the worst possible place to try to gather information, but also sort of the best.

Too many people and too much movement. There were too many opportunities to say something completely normal that somehow sounded like an accusation.

"You start," Tara said, appearing at her passenger window and entirely too cheerful for someone who hadn't suggested the idea.

Maddie tightened her grip on the steering wheel. "No."

"Please? People like you," Tara begged.

"No," Maddie responded more definitively.

"You're the one who noticed things."

"I notice things silently," Maddie shot back. "That's the whole point."

The carline inched forward.

Parents stepped in and out of conversations, choreographed sequences as doors opened and closed, seat belts clicked, and engines purred. Names were called. Someone

laughed a little too loudly, the sound cutting through everything else.

Normal.

Almost.

Except it wasn't.

"You're overthinking it," Tara said. "Just... ask a question."

"What kind of question?" Maddie whined.

"A normal one."

"There is no normal version of this."

Before Maddie could argue further, Donna appeared at her driver's side window.

"Madison," Donna said, already leaning in like she'd been invited. "How are you holding up?"

It wasn't a question people usually asked her.

Not like that.

Was she asking because she cared, or did she just want information?

"I'm fine," Maddie said carefully.

Donna nodded, studying her face like she might find something useful there. "I can't believe it was Derek," she said, lowering her voice just enough to suggest this was still somehow private. "I mean, right there. In our neighborhood."

Maddie hesitated, then chose her words carefully. "Did you... know him well?" A slight influx in her voice.

There it was.

Too direct?

Maybe. She didn't know; she had never done this before.

Donna didn't seem to think so. "Not well," she said quickly. "But enough. You see someone every day, you start to feel like you know them."

Maddie nodded. That part was true.

"But I will say," Donna continued, leaning in slightly. "Lindsay might have."

Maddie's attention sharpened. "Oh?"

Donna glanced over her shoulder, lowering her voice further. "They talked. Enough that I noticed."

Across the lane, Lindsay stood exactly where she had been yesterday. Mid-conversation, slightly animated, fully engaged.

Comfortable.

"What kind of 'talked'?" Tara asked casually, appearing at Maddie's passenger window as though she'd always been there.

Donna shrugged. "Just... conversations. I don't know what about."

Maddie followed her gaze. She figured Donna knew more, but she wasn't going to push. Yet.

Lindsay laughed at something someone said, hand resting lightly on another parent's arm. Easy. Effortless.

Like nothing had changed.

An instant passed.

Silence. And then...

"And Mark," Donna added, almost as an afterthought. "He's been... quiet."

Maddie glanced toward him.

Still in the same spot.

Still not saying much.

"He's always quiet," Tara said.

Donna shook her head. "Not like this. I just... I'd think with his background, he'd have more to contribute. That's all."

That stuck.

"What do you mean?" Maddie asked.

Donna leaned in again, lowering her voice. "Usually, he at least... participates. This?" She gestured subtly toward him. "This is avoiding. It's like he's trying to steer the conversation away from it. He was a cop for Pete's sake... It's his time to shine!"

Tara interjected, "I've always wondered why they moved back."

Donna offered up her own thoughts on the matter, "I don't buy the whole being closer to family thing. I mean, her brother lived in St. Louis, too."

Maddie felt that settle somewhere uncomfortably familiar.

Donna gave a nod, clearly pleased to have something worth sharing. "Anyway," she said, straightening. "If you hear anything..."

"We will," Maddie said automatically. Tara nodded in agreement.

Because apparently, she was part of this now.

Donna moved on just as quickly as she'd arrived, already scanning for her next conversation.

Maddie exhaled slowly. "That felt like an interrogation," she muttered.

"You only asked one question," Tara laughed. "Donna took it from there."

"Progress," Maddie responded.

Maddie glanced back toward Lindsay.

Then toward Mark.

Then toward the rest of the line.

"I don't know what we're supposed to be looking for," she admitted.

Tara leaned against the car door, considering. "Something that doesn't fit," she suggested.

Maddie frowned slightly.

Because that was the problem.

Nothing fit.

Derek didn't fit.

Vanessa didn't fit.

This didn't fit.

Her eyes drifted back to the groups of parents, to the small conversations happening in clusters, to the way people leaned in and pulled back like information was something you could physically pass between them.

Vanessa would have noticed something.

The thought came quietly.

But it stayed.

"She wasn't just watching," Maddie said, almost to herself.

Tara looked at her. "Huh?"

Maddie shook her head slightly, still looking out at the carline. "She was paying attention. It's like what she was doing wasn't creepy, but it had this weird level of intensity."

A small distinction.

But it felt important.

And for the first time since all of this started, Maddie had the uncomfortable sense that whatever had ended in Vanessa's backyard started long before yesterday.

CHAPTER 12
FRIDAY | STORIES

BY THE TIME Maddie pulled back into the carline, she wasn't second-guessing it anymore.

The hesitation from yesterday, the awkwardness, the feeling that she was stepping into something she didn't belong in, had dulled just enough to make room for something else.

Focus.

If there were answers, they weren't going to come to her. She was going to have to go out and get them.

"You look determined," Tara said, sliding into the passenger seat like it had become routine.

"I am," Maddie replied, eyes already scanning the carline.

Tara followed her gaze. "Who are we interrogating today?"

"Lindsay."

Tara smiled. "Bold."

"Efficient."

On the sidewalk, Lindsay was exactly where she had been the days before. Mid-conversation, coffee in hand, sunglasses pushed up into her hair. She laughed easily, leaning in just

enough to stay engaged without committing too much of herself to any one person.

It looked natural, but Maddie doubted it came that way.

Maddie didn't wait this time. She parked and opened her door before she could talk herself out of it. Tara followed, matching her pace as they walked, weaving through the rows of cars.

Lindsay was heading home, but noticed them almost immediately. "Oh, good," she said, turning toward them like they'd just joined a conversation already in progress. "Tell me you've heard something new."

"Not really," Maddie said. "Just trying to understand everything."

Lindsay nodded quickly. "Same. I mean, it's just... none of it makes any sense."

She said it easily.

Too easily.

"Did you know Derek well?" Tara asked, casual but direct. "I mean, outside of carline?"

Lindsay hesitated.

Just for a second.

She looked down, hands clasped, fingers fidgeting.

"I mean... kind of," she said. "We talked."

Maddie didn't fill the silence.

She let it sit.

Tara and Maddie maintained their gaze at Lindsay, encouraging her to continue.

It was awkward now.

Lindsay shifted slightly, glancing past them toward the carline before coming back. "We worked together. A little."

There it was.

"Worked how?" Maddie asked. "I thought you worked at

The Pretty Petal." The quaint flower shop was on the waterfront, the same one owned by Mark and Sonja.

Lindsay took a deep breath, her lips pursed together, like she was deciding how much to say. "Yeah... I help out Mark and Sonja part-time. With Derek, it was some investments. Nothing huge. Just some family savings we were hoping to grow."

Maddie and Tara didn't respond. Hoping the silence would encourage Lindsay to say more.

"Okay, not nothing," she added quickly. "But it was supposed to be simple. Safe."

Tara tilted her head. "And?"

Lindsay gave a short, humorless laugh. "And then it wasn't."

Maddie felt something sharpen.

"He handled everything," Lindsay continued, talking a little faster now. "Said he had experience, connections... whatever. And at first, it looked fine. He said we'd start with a cautious, low-risk investment." She paused. "Then things started dropping." As did the tone of Lindsay's voice.

"What kind of things?" Maddie asked.

"Everything," Lindsay huffed. "Accounts, returns... all of it. And every time I asked, there was an explanation."

"What kind of explanation?" Tara pressed.

"Timing," Lindsay said immediately. "Market shifts. Money being tied up. Different accounts. Yada, yada, yada." She closed her eyes for a moment and inhaled. "I was foolish, and he had an excuse for everything!" She shook her head slightly. "It was never just one place. Everything was... spread out. That's what he said."

Maddie's stomach tightened.

"It didn't make any sense," Lindsay continued, her eyes watering a little.

A small silence settled between Lindsay and the women,

who were feeling more and more like the faux Hardy Boys by the minute.

"I lost a lot," Lindsay said, quieter now. "More than I should have trusted him with in the first place."

Not anger.

Not exactly.

Something closer to embarrassment.

"I feel so stupid. But I wasn't the only one. Jared's furious, he'd probably be divorcing me if it wasn't just *my* savings."

"I'm so sorry," Maddie said, genuinely feeling sorry for the situation Derek had put Lindsay in.

Lindsay shrugged, but it felt smaller this time. "Yeah. Me too." She straightened slightly, like she was resetting herself. "I just think," she said, her tone shifting, "if anyone had a reason to be upset with him..."

She let the sentence trail off, but Maddie held her gaze. "You?" she asked.

Lindsay blinked, then laughed lightly.

"No," she said quickly. "I mean, not like that."

Too quick.

"I was mad," she admitted. "Of course I was. But I'm not..." she gestured vaguely. "A murderer," she finished this thought as a whisper. "I only invested a couple thousand; others did a lot more."

Maddie nodded slowly.

Because that part felt true.

"Did you talk to him recently?" Tara asked.

Lindsay hesitated, longer this time.

"A couple of weeks ago," she said. "Just to check in."

"And?" Maddie asked.

Lindsay glanced away briefly, like she was replaying it. "He said things were stabilizing," she said. "That everything was fine."

Maddie and Tara exchanged a quick look.

"Did you believe him?" Tara asked.

Lindsay smiled, but it didn't reach her eyes. "No."

The moment was ending.

"Well," Lindsay said, stepping back slightly, slipping back into something more polished, "if you hear anything..." She mimed making a phone call with her hand.

"We will," Maddie said.

They walked back toward the car in silence.

"That was... a lot," Tara said once they arrived at the car.

Maddie didn't answer right away; her eyes stayed on the carline.

On Lindsay.

On the way, she had already folded back into her walk home as if nothing had happened.

"She hated him," Tara added.

"Yeah," Maddie said. "Wouldn't you?"

"Oh yeah. I'd kill him! But not, like, literally."

"He kept it complicated," Maddie said slowly.

Tara frowned. "So people wouldn't question it?"

"That's what I'm thinking too. I wonder if someone did."

Maddie's gaze drifted. To Mark, to Donna, to everyone else.

To the quiet movement of people who all seemed to know each other just enough.

Maddie opened her car door, sat inside, and exhaled slowly, leaning back against her seat. Tara slid in next to her.

"This wasn't random," Maddie said.

Tara followed her gaze. "No," she agreed.

And this time, it didn't feel like a guess.

It felt like the beginning of an answer.

After all, they had their first suspect.

CHAPTER 13
FRIDAY | BALANCE

BY THE TIME the house was quiet, Maddie was running on fumes.

Not the chaotic, overstimulated kind that usually came with the end of the day, but something sharper. Focused. Awake in a way she hadn't felt in a while.

Lennon had finally settled in after the usual rotation of meds, stories, reassurance, one more kiss, and another one just in case. His image on the phone screen monitor, the small blue glow of his Minions nightlight, steady and familiar.

Kent was already in bed when Maddie entered, propped up against the headboard, scrolling through his phone.

He glanced up as she shut the door behind her. "You're late," he said, not accusing. Just noticing.

Maddie shrugged, pulling her t-shirt over her head and tossing it toward a chair, and reaching for her pajamas. "Lost track of time."

Kent watched her for a second. "That's new."

She paused halfway through pulling back the covers. "What is?"

"You. Losing track of time and not being stressed about it."

Maddie slid into bed, exhaling as she settled in. "I'm always stressed."

"Facts. But this is different."

"Huh?" She turned her head slightly, studying him. "Different how?"

Kent set his phone down on his chest. "You've been talking about this all night."

Maddie blinked. "I have not."

"You have," he said, a smirk forming. "Carline. The group chat. Derek. Vanessa. All of it."

Maddie opened her mouth to argue, then stopped. "Okay, maybe a little."

Kent let out a quiet breath, not quite a laugh. "More than a little."

She shifted onto her side, facing him now. "It's just…" She hesitated, trying to find the right way to explain something that didn't fully make sense even to her. "It doesn't add up."

Kent frowned slightly. "A man died, Maddie."

"I know," she said quickly. "I know that. I'm not..." She stopped again, pressing her lips together. "That's not what I mean."

"Then what do you mean?"

Maddie stared at the ceiling for a second before answering. "I mean, the story doesn't make sense. Everyone's acting like it's simple. Vanessa did it; she ran, end of story. But I doubt it's that simple."

Kent was quiet for a moment. "It never is. But you did find him at her house."

"I know," Maddie stated softly

"She's missing."

"I know," Maddie whispered this time.

"And you don't think that's relevant?"

Maddie turned her head back toward him. "Definitely relevant. I just don't think it's the whole picture."

Kent studied her for a moment, like he was trying to

decide how seriously to take what she was saying. "And you're planning to... what? Go all Nancy Drew and figure it out for the police?"

Maddie hesitated. A smirk. "Tara's helping... We're positioning ourselves more along the lines of the Hardy Boys."

"Of course, Tara's involved," Kent replied, scoffing.

"We're just talking to people," she said finally, casually. "Trying to understand what actually happened."

Kent let out a slow breath. "That sounds like trying to figure it out."

"It's not," she said, a little too quickly. "It's just... being aware."

"Mm."

She narrowed her eyes slightly. "Don't 'mm' me."

"I'm not 'mm'-ing you. I'm just... trying to understand why you're involved."

There it was.

The question she knew was coming.

Maddie looked away, her gaze drifting toward the faint glow of the monitor. "I don't know."

That wasn't entirely true.

But it was close enough.

Because the truth was—

It felt good.

She had a purpose outside of being *Lennon's Mom.*

Not the situation.

Not what had happened.

But the thinking. The paying attention. The connecting pieces that no one else seemed to notice.

For the first time in a long time, her brain wasn't stuck in routines and reminders and getting ahead of the next meltdown before it happened.

It was... engaged.

"I just," Maddie started again, quieter this time. "I feel like there's something there. And everyone's just skipping over it."

Kent shifted slightly, turning more toward her. "And that's your responsibility?"

"No," she said immediately.

Then, after a beat...

"But if I can see it..."

She didn't finish.

She didn't need to.

Kent was quiet for a long moment.

"You're allowed to be interested," he said finally. "That's not what I'm worried about."

Maddie glanced at him. "Then what are you worried about?"

"That it turns into something else. Something bigger than you think it is."

She softened a little, reaching over and nuzzling into his arm. "I'm not quitting my job and becoming a detective, if that's what you're worried about."

"Good. Because I don't think we budgeted for that."

A small smile pulled at her mouth. "Relax. I know I have actual work to do."

"Do you?" he asked lightly.

She nudged him again. "Don't start."

Kent smiled, but it faded quickly into something more thoughtful. "Just... be careful. Okay?"

"I will."

And she meant it.

As she rolled over and settled into her pillow, the quiet of the room settling around them, her mind didn't slow.

It sharpened.

Derek.

Vanessa.

The way people talked.

The way they didn't.

The way things seemed normal.

And all the ways they didn't.

There was something there.

She was sure of it.

And for the first time in a long time, Maddie wasn't just getting through the day.

She was looking forward to it.

CHAPTER 14
SATURDAY | FOOTAGE

GREG BENNETT.

If there was one person in the neighborhood who always knew what was going on, it was Greg.

Not in a loud, Donna-with-a-group-chat kind of way.

Quieter.

Moreso, intentional.

He ran the neighborhood watch, though it wasn't the kind of neighborhood that needed one.

At least not until recently.

He did, however, take it seriously. Cameras. Alerts. Emails no one really reads.

Maddie hadn't paid much attention to any of it.

Until the night Lennon got out.

She could still feel that moment if she let herself think about it too long. The panic, the not knowing, the way her heart had dropped into her stomach when she realized the front door was open.

Greg had been the one who found him.

A grainy clip from his motion-activated camera. Lennon

was on the sidewalk, barefoot, wandering just far enough to matter.

A knock at the door minutes later.

Calm. Steady. Like it wasn't the worst thing that could have happened.

Maddie had given him a $50 gift card, which he tried to decline. "Just doing my part." It didn't feel like enough. What do you give a guy who kept your kid safe when you weren't?

And then yesterday, he had been there, too.

Arriving alongside the police.

Before the questions.

Standing just beyond the tape.

Talking quietly to one of the officers, as if he belonged there.

Like he already knew something.

She looked down at her phone.

If anyone had seen something, it would be Greg.

She stood at the kitchen counter, staring at her phone, rereading the same text she'd typed three times and still hadn't sent.

> **Maddie**
> Hi, Greg! I have a quick question about your Ring camera.

She deleted it.

Too vague.

She tried again.

> **Maddie**
> Hey! Random question. Did your cameras happen to catch anything the other day?

Delete.

Too obvious.

"Maddie."

She looked up.

Kent stood in the doorway, energy drink in hand, watching her with mild curiosity.

"You've been typing the same text for ten minutes," he said.

"I'm thinking," she replied.

"You're spiraling," Kent whispered sarcastically.

"I'm not spiraling."

"You're absolutely spiraling."

"It's what I do," she said with a smile. Maddie sighed, dropping her phone onto the counter. "I just need to ask Greg something."

"Then ask him."

"It's not that simple."

Kent took a sip of his coffee. "It's a text."

"It's not just a text. It feels nosy."

Kent raised an eyebrow. "You're asking about a camera, not asking him what he weighs."

Maddie opened her mouth to respond, then stopped. "Okay. Fair."

She picked up her phone again.

Typed.

Maddie
Hey, Greg! You around today?

Paused.

Then, before she could overthink it, she hit send.

She barely had time to set the phone back down before it buzzed in her hand.

Greg
All day. You doing okay? That had to be quite a shock on Monday.

Maddie blinked.

That was faster than expected.

She remembered that Greg was the first neighbor to show up after the police.

Maddie
Yeah, okay. Was wondering if your camera caught anything from that day?

Three dots appeared almost immediately.

Then disappeared.

Then came back again.

Kent leaned slightly against the counter, reading the response over her shoulder. "That seems like a good sign," he said.

"Or a bad one," Maddie muttered.

Her phone buzzed again.

Greg
It caught some stuff. Why?

Maddie's grip tightened slightly.

"Okay," she said quietly. "That's… something."

Kent tilted his head. "What kind of 'something'?"

She typed quickly.

Maddie
Would you mind showing me?

This time, the pause was longer.

Long enough for Maddie to feel it.

Then...

Greg
Come on over.

Maddie looked up at Kent. "Looks like I'm going to Greg's place," she said with a cautious smile and more glee than she intended.

Kent didn't immediately respond.

"Maddie," he said carefully, "this is where I remind you that you are not actually part of this investigation. You are not the police, and you are not a private investigator."

"I know," she said quickly. "I'm just... looking."

He held her gaze for a second longer.

Then nodded.

"Just looking," he repeated.

Maddie grabbed her keys and headed to the door.

Joon's nails clicked excitedly against the floor as soon as she saw the movement.

"Oh no," Maddie said.

Too late.

Joon was already at the door, tail wagging like this was the best decision anyone had ever made.

"Fine," Maddie muttered, grabbing the leash. "You can come. But you're not helping."

The late morning air was warm without being hot, the kind of quiet that only existed on weekends. No buses. No rush. Just the occasional sound of someone mowing a lawn and children playing. As an added bonus, Lennon spent the first six hours of the day at a social group for kids with disabilities. It was supposed to help Lennon learn appropriate behaviors and life skills and to improve his communication. He loved it, called it "playroom."

Greg's house sat just a few doors down, familiar in the way all of them were. Similar layout. Same driveway. Same carefully maintained front yard.

And directly across the street from Vanessa.

Maddie hesitated for half a second before ringing the bell.

The door opened almost immediately.

Greg looked just like he always did. Casual, guarded, but not unfriendly. He donned a Tommy Bahama shirt, cargo shorts, and flip-flops. He embodied all that you would expect from a seventy-year-old retired postal worker.

"Maddie," he said cheerfully. "Hello."

"Hi," she replied, suddenly aware of Joon attempting to push her way inside. "Sorry. She thinks everywhere is her house. She'll be fine staying out here on the porch."

Greg glanced down as Joon leaned enthusiastically into his leg.

"Nah... she's welcome inside. She can't do any more damage than the grandkids," he said, reaching down to give her a quick pat. "She seems harmless."

"She is. Mostly." A wink.

He stepped back, holding the door open. "You want to see the footage?"

Straight to the point.

Maddie appreciated that.

"Yeah," she said.

Greg guided her into the living room, where a laptop sat open on the coffee table. "I didn't think much of it at first," he said, sitting down and pulling up a video. "Just normal movement. People coming and going."

A moment passed.

Maddie stepped closer, her attention sharpening.

"But then," Greg continued, pausing the screen and rewinding slightly, "after everything, I went back and looked again... To see if I missed something."

He hit play.

The grainy black-and-white footage showed the quiet street, still and uneventful. A timestamp blinked in the corner.

Then, movement.

A car pulled up in front of the Sams's house.

Maddie leaned in slightly. She recognized the car from the carline.

"That's him," Greg said. "The dead guy."

"Derek," Maddie replied softly.

Even through the low-quality footage, she recognized him immediately. The way he moved. The way he parked. Blocking Vanessa's SUV in the driveway. And stepping out like he had somewhere specific to be.

"What time is that?" she asked.

Greg pointed to the corner of the screen. "Just before six."

Maddie's mind started turning.

A few moments later, Evan's truck pulled up, and he carefully lowered his lawnmower down to the sidewalk, and he started in the front yard. Mowing.

In addition to being an aide at the school and a student, Evan also made extra money on the side mowing lawns around town.

The footage jumped. Minutes passed in seconds. The street stayed quiet. Empty. Still.

Eventually, Evan left, but everything else remained the same.

Nothing but Derek's car, Vanessa's SUV, and the Sams's house on the screen.

Maddie's heart was pounding, just knowing something so macabre could be happening just off-screen.

"Keep watching," Greg said, his voice low.

Another jump.

A large stretch of nothing.

Then, a flicker of movement.

"Two o'clock," Greg said.

Maddie leaned closer.

"Is that...?"

"Vanessa."

The figure moved quickly, just barely visible as she crossed from the side of the house toward the front.

Not running.

Not frantic.

She walked to the mailbox, placed some envelopes inside, and lifted the red flag.

She returned a moment later, carrying a sleeping Ellie. She moved carefully, placing the girl in the backseat of Derek's car before heading back inside once more.

A final trip.

She came out with two bags and her purse.

Got into the car and drove away.

"Two-oh-seven," Greg said.

They watched as the car disappeared out of frame.

"Do they come back?" Maddie asked.

"Nope," he said with finality.

Maddie swallowed.

The room felt quieter somehow.

She straightened slightly, her mind trying to piece it together.

Her palms were sweaty as she wiped them on her pants.

She replayed it in her head.

Derek arrives.

Vanessa leaves.

But that wasn't the whole story.

It couldn't be.

After all, there were nearly eight hours unaccounted for.

"Can I see it again?" she whispered.

Greg nodded, scrolling back through the footage.

This time, Maddie watched differently.

Not just what was happening, but how it was happening.

She pulled out her phone, jotting down times and small details as the video played.

Derek didn't hesitate when he arrived.

He intentionally blocked Vanessa's SUV.

Vanessa didn't panic when she left.

Heck, she even dropped something into the mailbox.

Nothing about it felt random.

It didn't necessarily feel planned, but there was structure to it.

Maybe that was just Vanessa's way.

Poised, even under pressure.

Maddie exhaled slowly.

"That flicker of light... around 8? What was that?" Maddie asked.

"Just the neighbor's headlights. He comes home every night at the same time."

Nothing unusual about that.

Normal.

But clearly something *had* happened.

"Thank you," she said. Then, after a thoughtful pause, "Did you show this to the police?"

Greg nodded. "Yeah. They are trying to track down the car and the Sams family."

Maddie gave a small, distracted nod.

Greg recorded everything.

Vanessa remembered everything.

Now, they had more than just stories.

They had a timeline.

And a second suspect.

CHAPTER 15
SUNDAY | SHIFT

SUNDAY DIDN'T FEEL like a day of rest.

Lennon's social group had been canceled. Which meant the investigation was temporarily on pause.

Maddie stood in her kitchen, staring down at her phone while Joon paced slow, lazy circles at her feet, and the hum of cartoons drifted in from the living room. Kent had Lennon and Piper set up with snacks, screens, and what sounded like a surprisingly peaceful stretch of cooperation.

It wouldn't last, but for now, it was holding.

Tara dropped Piper off in an attempt to grocery shop in peace. With Piper by her side, she'd spend half the time saying "No" to whatever sugary, carb-laden snacks Piper took off the shelves and tossed into the cart. It was easier this way.

Her phone buzzed.

3rd Grade Group Chat

Donna
Police update. They are officially looking for Vanessa and Ellie. They believe she fled after the incident.

Maddie read it twice. The incident.

Then a third time.

Lindsay
That makes sense.

Parent #1
OMG...

Parent #2
Fled?

Chloe
That's just not who Vanessa is.

Mark
It's just protocol.

Silence.

Maddie's jaw tightened slightly.

No mention of Derek beyond the obvious implication of an incident. No mention of anything else. No questions. No uncertainty.

Just a direction.

"They've already decided," she muttered. "It can't be that cut and dry."

From the living room, Kent called out, "You talking to the dog or me?"

"Both," she said, grabbing her keys off the counter. "I'm running out for a bit. Can you watch the kids?"

A pause. "Running where?" he asked dryly.

"Errands," she said, a little too quickly.

Another pause. Longer this time. Kent knew her well enough to know exactly what she was doing. "I'll watch the kids, but you be careful."

Maddie responded, "Of course I will."

She slipped out the front door before he could ask

anything else.

The school parking lot was empty.

Quiet in a way it never was during the week. No cars lining up. No clusters of parents. No Donna projecting her voice across the asphalt, half hanging out of her car window.

Just stillness.

Maddie spotted Evan near the side entrance, sitting on the curb with his phone in his hand, one earbud in, one dangling loose. He looked up as she approached, a little taken aback.

She knew exactly where to find Evan in the small town, and he was exactly the person she was looking for.

"Oh. Hey, Mrs. Carter," he said, pulling the other earbud out. "Hi."

"Hi," Maddie said, offering a small smile. "Sorry, I didn't mean to interrupt."

"No, you're good." He stood, brushing his hands on his shorts. "How's Lennon doing today?"

"He's good, he was a handful yesterday, but we're good today."

"That's our Lennon," he chuckled.

"I just... I had a question. About Vanessa's house." Maddie second-guessed herself as soon as she started.

"Okay..."

"You mow her lawn, right?"

Evan nodded. "Yeah. Still do. Well, maybe. I don't know."

Maddie shifted her weight slightly. "Do you remember Monday night?"

"Uh, yeah," he said. "I go out on Mondays. Same four houses every week."

"And hers is one of them?" Maddie already knew the answer; she remembered the freshly cut lawn, the smell of grass. Not to mention the video footage.

"Yeah," he said again, more certain. "I was there around...

Six-ish? Maybe? She's the third house on my route, and I start as soon as school lets out."

Maddie's focus sharpened. "And everything looked," a brief pause, "normal?"

"Yeah," he said, brow furrowing slightly like he was replaying it. "Totally normal. Yard was fine. Lights were on, I think. Not much to notice. She actually came outside and talked to me for a minute."

"She did?" Maddie blurted the question louder than intended. This was not something they saw on the video.

"Yeah. She usually doesn't," he said, almost apologetically. "She's nice, just... quick. You know?"

Maddie nodded slowly. She did know. "What did she say?"

Evan shrugged. "Nothing big. Just wanted to pay me this month and next up front. She usually pays at the end of the month."

"Did she say why?"

"Not really. Just said she might be out of town, wanted to make sure I got it." He hesitated. "She seemed... I don't know. A little distracted, I guess. I think she had a friend over. There was another car by the driveway that wasn't normally there. I heard it might have been Derek's."

Maddie didn't speak right away. She was processing that information. What would make Vanessa break her routine?

"Everything was fine when you left?" she asked.

"Yeah," Evan said firmly. "Totally fine. At least outside."

Maddie nodded. "Okay. Thank you."

"Is..." he started, then stopped. "Is everything okay?"

Maddie gave him a small, practiced smile. "Yeah. Just trying to make sense of things."

He nodded, though he didn't look entirely convinced.

Maddie turned and walked back toward her car.

Monday night.

Everything seemed fine.

. . .

Chloe was harder to approach.

Maddie knew she ran in the early afternoons at Riverview Park, so once she eyed Chloe's car, she pulled into the parking lot and waited.

Five minutes passed. Ten.

No Chloe.

It was just a matter of waiting.

Finally, Chloe rounded the corner, slowing to a jog and then a walk. She sat down on a nearby bench and drank some water from the yellow Hydro Flask at her hip.

Maddie hesitated before walking over.

"Hey," she said.

Chloe looked up, a little surprised to see Maddie's familiar face. "Hi."

"Mind if I sit?"

Chloe reluctantly gestured beside her. "Go ahead."

Maddie sat, hands resting loosely in her lap.

For a second, neither of them spoke.

"You're fast."

Chloe let out a soft chuckle, "Thanks. Training for Boston."

"The Marathon?! That's huge."

"It's always been on my bucket list, and I didn't qualify this year," Chloe responded, a hint of sadness in her voice.

"Well, I'm sure you will soon," Maddie responded and let a moment of comfortable silence sit between them. "Everyone's talking."

Chloe gave a small, humorless smile. "They always are."

"This feels... different."

"Because it is, this time someone died." Chloe's voice was flat.

Maddie studied her for a moment. "You and Vanessa were close." Not a question.

Chloe didn't deny it. "Are close. We are friends."

That shifted something.

Maddie leaned back slightly. "She doesn't seem like... what people are saying."

Chloe's expression didn't change, but something in her posture did. Subtle and firm. "She's not," Chloe responded with quiet conviction. Not defensive, just certain.

Maddie chose her next words carefully. "Then why does it look like she ran?"

Chloe looked out toward the street, her gaze distant for a second before returning. "When you've lived through certain things," she said slowly, "you don't wait around to see how they play out."

Maddie's stomach tightened.

"What kind of things?"

Chloe shook her head once. "Not mine to share. But I will say this," she added, her voice softer now. "Everything she did... I'm sure it was about Ellie. People keep calling her controlling. Careful. Intense. But no one's asking why."

Maddie didn't respond.

Chloe stood, brushing off her leggings."I'm not going to speculate about her. Not like everyone else is." Then, after a second… "If something happened," she added, glancing back, "I don't think it started that night." And just like that, she started walking away. "See you tomorrow, Madison."

"Bye."

Maddie sat there for a moment longer.

Letting that settle.

By the time Maddie pulled into the parking lot of The Pretty Petal at 1:00, her phone buzzed.

Tara
You're interrogating people WITHOUT ME??
😠

Maddie sighed, already knowing how this was going to go.

Maddie
I talked to Evan and Chloe. Neither were interrogations.

Three dots appeared immediately.

Tara
Rude. Where are you?

Maddie hesitated, then typed.

Maddie
Pretty Petal

The reply came almost instantly.

Tara
Oh no you don't! Do. Not. Start.
Without. Me.

Maddie glanced toward the shop doors, then back at her phone.

Too late.

Maddie's eagerness was getting the better of her.

The bell above the door chimed softly as she stepped inside.

The shop smelled like fresh lavender and roses and damp greenery, cool and quiet compared to the heat outside. Buckets of flowers lined the walls, soft music humming somewhere in the background.

Mark stood behind the counter, trimming the ends of a

bundle of white lilies with careful precision. He looked up as she approached.

"Good day, Madison," he said. He set the shears down, wiping his hands on a towel. "What brings you in today?"

Maddie glanced briefly around the shop before answering. "I wanted to order something. For Derek."

Something flickered across his face. Distaste? Maybe. But it was gone almost immediately.

"Yeah," he said. "It's tragic. We've had a few orders already. Service is next weekend."

"Where's Sonja?" Maddie asked.

"She's usually in the shop on weekends, but she's at her brother's this week. St. Louis for her nephew's baptism. So you get me." He chortled. "Arrangement? Or maybe something potted?"

"Potted," Maddie said. "Nothing over the top." She liked the idea of something the Holloway family could keep, something that wouldn't wilt away after the service.

He nodded, already turning to pull some ideas together. Efficient. Focused. "You knew him?" he asked, not looking up.

"Not really," Maddie said. "Carline."

"Yeah. Same."

Maddie watched him for a moment. "You were around him more than most, though, right? Not too many dads in carline."

Mark shrugged slightly. "We crossed paths. Kids played soccer together, co-ed league. Sonja usually works the day shift, and Derek's wife travels a lot."

"For work?" Maddie inquired.

Before Mark could respond, the bell above the door chimed again.

"Wow," Tara's voice cut in as she walked up beside Maddie. "You really were going to do this without me." A confused expression played on Mark's face.

Maddie didn't look at her. "You didn't say don't go inside."

Tara smirked, then turned her attention to Mark like she'd been there the whole time. "Hi," she said brightly. "We're ordering funeral flowers for Derek and asking mildly invasive questions."

Mark's mouth twitched slightly. Not quite a smile. "Good to know."

Tara leaned casually against the counter, cutting right to the chase. "He didn't seem like someone who had enemies, but Lindsay said otherwise..."

"In the group chat," Maddie added.

Mark's hands didn't stop moving. "Most people don't," he said, "have real enemies, that is."

"Lindsay said they did some business together," Maddie added.

That got a reaction. Small and subtle, but it was there.

"Did she?" Mark said. A small laugh.

Tara tilted her head. "You didn't know that?" She was taking her role in this interrogation a little too seriously.

Mark finally looked up. "Derek did a lot of things. He had different investment opportunities every day of the week, depending on who you ask."

That didn't exactly match what Lindsay had said. But she had an inkling that Mark was more perceptive.

Maddie felt that click quietly into place. "You think people are jumping to conclusions?" she asked.

Mark let out a slow breath. "I think people like answers. Even if they're the wrong ones."

"So, you think they're the wrong ones?" Tara quipped.

Mark didn't respond. He just kept pulling together options for the funeral. "Did you want the flowers delivered directly to the funeral home?"

"Ummm... Yeah. That'll work," Maddie answered.

"And Vanessa?" Tara questioned.

A pause.

Brief. Controlled.

"She keeps to herself," he said.

Maddie thought of Chloe. "That's not really what I've heard," Maddie said lightly.

Mark's hands stilled for half a second before continuing. "People hear what they want to hear," he said.

"She doesn't seem like someone who would just..." Maddie trailed off.

"Disappear?" Mark finished. "No, she doesn't." He met her gaze evenly. "But then again, people leave all the time. You'd be surprised how easy it is."

There it was again. That certainty.

Maddie forced a small nod. "Maybe."

"Anything else?"

Maddie hesitated, but Tara beat her to it.

"Nope," Tara said. "We've taken up enough of your time."

Maddie shot her a look. She had a million more questions.

Tara just smiled.

Mark got their approval on the flowers and slid them a condolence card to complete. "I'll be sure everything looks perfect for the service."

They paid, thanked him, and stepped back out into the sunlight as the door chimed behind them.

For a second, neither of them spoke.

"Well," Tara said, adjusting her sunglasses. "That was weird."

Maddie let out a slow breath. "Evan was normal," she said.

"Okay."

"Chloe..." she hesitated. "Protective."

"Of Vanessa?"

Maddie nodded. She glanced back toward the shop. "I don't think they're involved."

"And Mark?" Tara didn't hesitate.

"Off."

"Off enough to get put on the suspect list?"

"Absolutely."

"That makes three."

Maddie exhaled, pulling her keys from her pocket. "They're looking for Vanessa," she said.

Tara stood on the sidewalk nearby. "Yeah. Because it looks obvious."

That was the problem; it did look obvious.

But as Maddie slid into her driver's seat, one thought settled in, clear and steady. "I don't think she ran."

Tara looked at her, questioning.

Maddie started the car. "I think she left."

CHAPTER 16
MONDAY | TENSION

MONDAY FELT LOUDER THAN USUAL. Not in volume. In awareness.

Maddie eased into the carline, her usual spot with the lineup half-filled, engines idling, doors opening and closing in a rhythm that should have felt familiar.

It didn't.

People were watching.

Not openly. Not obviously.

But enough.

Conversations paused just slightly as she pulled forward. A glance here. A second look there.

She hadn't imagined it.

She was the one who found the body.

Either word got around, or her car had something inappropriate written on the passenger side.

Why were they all looking at *her*?

"Okay, celebrity," Tara said, slipping into the passenger seat without invitation. "You can't just go rogue all weekend and not expect consequences."

Maddie didn't look at her. "I talked to three people."

"You talked to *Evan*." Of course, the whole school knows.

"He was sitting alone."

"That is not the point."

"You think they're looking at me because I asked some questions? Plus," Maddie finally glanced over. "You were there for our visit with Mark."

"Barely," Tara said. "And I had to chase you down like I was in some kind of low-budget detective movie."

Maddie huffed a small laugh despite herself. "What did you think?"

Tara didn't hesitate. "Mark is weird."

"Not helpful."

"No, I mean it," Tara said, leaning back. "Not loud weird. Quiet weird. Like... he's already decided what this is."

"Maybe supercop already cracked the case. Shall we invite him to join our little gang?"

"Let's wait until we decide if he's guilty of something."

Maddie nodded slowly. "Good call."

A sharp voice cut across the carline.

"Madison." A sing-song voice called out. "Madison Carter! Yoo-Hoo!"

Donna.

Of course.

She approached like she always did, with confidence and directness, and was already mid-conversation before she reached the car.

"Have you heard?" Donna asked.

"Heard what?" Tara jumped in.

Donna lowered her voice slightly, though not enough to suggest actual discretion. "Police were here this morning. Talking to staff."

Maddie's attention sharpened. "About what?"

"Derek," Donna said. "They're asking about who he talked to. Sign-ins. His kid's attendance. Everything."

"They think Vanessa did it?" Tara said.

Donna nodded. "They're focusing on finding her. But they're still asking questions."

Maddie's mind started turning.

Good. They should be.

"Just thought you'd want to know..."

Apparently, she was getting a reputation for being nosy.

A car door slammed a few spaces ahead.

Maddie's gaze shifted automatically.

Ryan Patel.

He stood beside his SUV, one hand on the door, as his twin boys climbed out. One moving quickly, already halfway toward the sidewalk, the other lingering, just a second longer.

"Arjun," Ryan said, not raising his voice. "Wait."

The boy paused. He glared at his father.

"Sorry... AJ," Ryan corrected himself smoothly, glancing toward the line of parents.

The moment was small and easy to miss, but Maddie didn't miss it.

"That's him," Tara murmured.

"Ryan? I know... I'm just not friends with people; I know who they are."

Tara nodded. "Factory guy. Logistics or something. Smart. Quiet."

Maddie watched as Ryan adjusted his son's backpack, saying something low and quick before sending both boys toward the entrance.

Efficient and controlled.

"Come on," Tara said.

Maddie didn't argue.

"Hey, Ryan," she called as they approached.

Ryan turned, already composed. "Good morning."

"Hi," Maddie said. "We were just, erm, talking to Donna. About, well, everything."

A flicker of recognition.

Awareness.

"Yeah," he said. "You've been talking to a lot of people."

Maddie brushed it off.

"You knew Derek outside of school, right?" Tara asked, skipping the warm-up.

Ryan's expression didn't change. "A little. Work-related."

"What kind of work?" Maddie asked.

"Finance," he said. "He handled some things for Bayline Industrial through his company."

"His company," Tara repeated.

Ryan nodded once. "He helped with some investments. Growth accounts. Employee 401(k) type stuff."

Maddie tilted her head slightly. "So... you didn't interact much?"

"Not really," Ryan said. Then, almost as an afterthought... "He was around some."

Around how? What did he mean by that? Maddie asked herself.

"Do you remember Monday night?" she asked.

Ryan's gaze shifted briefly toward the school doors, then back. "Not specifically. Why?"

"Just trying to piece things together," Tara said lightly.

Ryan gave a small, polite smile. "I think that's the police's job."

There it was.

Boundary set.

"Of course," Maddie said quickly. "Just... small town, you know?"

Ryan nodded, already stepping back. "Yeah. Exactly."

And just like that, the conversation was over.

"Well," Tara said under her breath as they walked back. "That was nothing."

Maddie didn't respond right away.

Because it wasn't *nothing*.

It was... contained. Too contained.

. . .

U-Brewed was louder than usual. Not chaotic. Just busy enough that conversations blended into a steady hum. Maddie and Tara sat near the window, their drinks sweating onto the table.

"I'm just saying," Tara said, stirring her drink, "Someone knows more than they're letting on..."

Maddie reached out, tapping her arm lightly. "Wait."

Tara blinked. "What?"

Maddie didn't answer. She tilted her head slightly, listening. "That's Ryan's wife," she whispered, head indicating the table behind them.

There, two women sat close together, voices low, but not quiet enough.

"… I told him to stop."

Maddie stilled.

Tara followed her gaze immediately, shifting just enough to listen without turning.

"I'm serious, Anika," the other woman said. "You should have said something."

There it was.

"… I didn't know," Anika said. "Not like that."

"Come on," her friend said, somewhat accusingly. "You said he was texting you."

"He was," Anika snapped, then lowered her voice. "But Derek wasn't like that. Not at first."

Maddie picked up her drink, holding it near her mouth, not sipping.

"You told Ryan?" the friend asked.

A pause.

"He told me to let it go," Anika said.

"That's it?!" She was noticeably surprised.

"What was I supposed to do?" Anika said, frustration creeping in. "Make it a thing? It was already complicated… and then everything happened."

Silence.

"Ryan was already upset about the situation Derek had put his business in. I think he didn't want to deal with one more thing."

"I heard he was involved in a lot of people's finances."

"You did?"

"After he died... people just started talking. A lot of people in Dogwood Bay did not like that man."

Maddie slowly set her drink down.

Tara's eyes met hers.

No words.

They didn't need them.

They had another suspect.

By the time pickup rolled around, Maddie's head was full.

Evan.

Five-thirty. Six. Paid in advance. Normal.

Chloe.

Everything Vanessa did was about Ellie.

Ryan.

Work. Accounting. Derek's firm. His wife.

A return visit to U-Brewed, and Maddie made it to Lennon's OT appointment with five minutes to spare.

He adored his therapist, Mister Jerry. Maddie worked from her car while Lennon partook in the familiar, structured activities. Soft instructions paired with big movements. The steady rhythm of a place designed to hold things together, and a plan in place in case it fell apart. The car was where she caught up on emails and writing tasks. That is, when she wasn't distracted by other things.

. . .

As they turned down the street to head home, Maddie spotted Evan unloading his mower at Vanessa's.

He looked up when he saw her and waved.

She pulled to the curb and rolled down the window. "Hi, Evan. Quick question."

He smiled slightly. "Yeah, figured."

"Monday," she said. "When you left here, what time was it exactly?"

Evan shifted his weight, thinking. "Um... probably close to seven. Her yard isn't that big."

Maddie's focus sharpened. "And when did you talk to her?"

"It was out back," he answered. "So about halfway through."

Maddie nodded slowly. "And Derek's car was already there?" She was asking questions she already knew the answers to.

"Yeah," Evan said. "I didn't know it was his at the time. I only realized later… after everything."

That settled something.

"She seemed normal when you talked?" Maddie asked.

"Yeah," he said. Then hesitated. "Just, like I mentioned, a little distracted."

There it was again.

Maddie nodded. "Okay. Thank you."

"No problem," he said. "Everything okay?"

Maddie gave the same answer she always did, regardless of who was doing the asking. "Fine."

Back at home, Maddie set her phone on the counter and put Tara on speaker as she prepped snacks and lunches for the week. Something she'd completely forgotten to do on Sunday.

Silence hung between them for a moment.

"You're thinking something," Tara said. "Just say it."

Maddie wiped her hands on a towel. "Evan got there around six," she said. "Derek was already there."

"Yeah. We knew that."

"Yeah," Maddie said slowly. "But that means whatever happened... didn't happen right when he got there."

Tara went quiet. "What do you mean?"

Maddie exhaled, staring down at the counter. "Everyone's focused on Derek showing up. Vanessa leaving. The body." She shook her head. "That's the middle."

"He was there for over an hour before, ya know..."

Another pause.

Longer this time.

"So what's the beginning?" Tara asked.

Maddie didn't answer right away.

Because she didn't know yet.

But she knew one thing.

They weren't asking the right questions.

And somewhere between the timeline, Chloe's quiet defense, Ryan's too-clean answers, and everything else - something wasn't lining up.

Maddie finally said, quieter this time, "This didn't start with Derek's death… It started before he ever pulled into that driveway."

CHAPTER 17
TUESDAY | STATIC

DONNA DIDN'T WAIT for an invitation.

She rarely did.

Maddie had barely put the car in park before Donna appeared at her window, coffee in hand, sunglasses perched on her head as if she had somewhere more important to be, but lucky for them, had chosen this instead.

"Well," she said, leaning in slightly. "You've been busy."

Maddie didn't bother pretending. "You've been watching."

Donna smiled. "Of course I have. Don't I *always*?" She knew who she was, and Maddie appreciated that about Donna.

Tara slid into the passenger seat. "We were just saying how much we missed your updates."

"Oh, I have updates," Donna said quickly. "You're going to love this."

That wasn't a reassuring sentence.

Donna lowered her voice. Not enough to make it private, just enough to make it feel like it was. "Ryan Patel. Not as put together as he looks."

Maddie's attention sharpened. "Oh?"

Donna took a sip of her coffee like she was pacing herself. "Marital issues. Have been for a while."

Tara raised an eyebrow. "Define 'a while.'"

"Before this," Donna said. "Before Derek."

That mattered.

Maddie glanced at Tara.

Not motive.

Not yet.

"But," Donna added, leaning in a little closer now, "Derek didn't help."

There it was.

Maddie kept her voice even. "What do you mean?"

Tara clasped her hands and rubbed them together, "Give us all the juicy details."

Donna gave her a look. A slight roll of the eyes directed at Tara. "Oh, come on. You didn't notice?"

"No," Maddie said flatly.

Tara nodded. "We're busy surviving our children." A laugh.

"He flirted with her. All the time."

"Anika?" Maddie asked.

"Yes," Donna said. "And not subtle."

Tara let out a quiet "huh."

Maddie's mind started filing it away.

Flirtation wasn't murder.

But it was friction.

"I saw it myself," Donna continued. "Pick-up, events, fundraisers... He always found a way to be near her."

"And Ryan?" Maddie asked.

Donna shrugged. "Hard to tell. He's not exactly... expressive."

That tracked.

"But if you're asking me," Donna said, straightening slightly, "that house has had issues long before Derek showed up."

Maddie nodded slowly.

That confirmed it.

Ryan wasn't new tension; he was ongoing tension.

"Anything else?" Tara asked.

Donna hesitated.

Which was new.

"Well," she said finally, "Vanessa didn't like him."

Maddie stilled. "Ryan?"

Donna shook her head. "Derek."

That made more sense.

"She kept her distance," Donna said. "Didn't engage. Which, honestly, made him try harder. He was trying to figure her out or something."

Maddie felt something shift.

Vanessa.

Not passive.

Intentional.

"Did they ever argue?" Maddie asked.

"Not that I saw," Donna said. "But you could tell."

"Tell what?"

Donna met her eyes. "She didn't trust him."

That sat heavier than everything else.

The bell rang in the distance, signaling the start of the school day.

Donna stepped back from the window. "Well," she said, like she hadn't just dropped something important, "keep me posted."

And just like that, she was gone.

Tara exhaled slowly. "Okay," she said. "So now we have flirting, marital problems, and... whatever that was."

"Vanessa didn't trust him," Maddie said quietly.

Tara glanced at her. "You think that matters?"

Maddie didn't answer right away.

Because it did.

She just didn't know how yet.

. . .

Ryan was harder to catch this time.

He stayed closer to his car, moving with the same quiet efficiency as before, ushering AJ and Michael out with minimal conversation.

Maddie didn't give herself time to hesitate.

"Ryan," she called.

He turned.

Polite. Composed. Already guarded.

"Hey," he said.

"Can we ask you something?" Tara said, stepping in beside Maddie.

A pause. Then a nod. "I don't think I can stop you."

Maddie didn't ease into it. "Derek flirted with your wife?"

Tara blinked.

Well, that was direct.

Ryan's expression didn't change immediately.

But something behind it did.

Tighter.

"People talk," he said.

"That's not a no," Tara pointed out.

Ryan let out a slow breath. "No," he said finally. "It's not."

Silence stretched for a beat.

"It was inappropriate," Ryan continued. "I addressed it."

"How?" Maddie asked.

"Directly," he said. "With him."

That was new. Someone who confronts problems head-on.

"And?" Tara asked.

Ryan's jaw shifted slightly. "He said it was harmless. That's usually how those conversations go."

Apparently, he had these conversations before. Was Ryan a jealous husband? Or was Anika a flirtatious spouse?

Maddie could picture both.

Easily.

"And your wife?" Maddie asked.

Ryan's gaze flickered briefly. "She handled it too."

Vague.

Again.

"Did it cause problems?" Tara asked.

Ryan gave a short, humorless smile. "It's really none of your business, but we had problems long before Derek."

That lined up with what Donna had said.

"But not the kind that end like this," he added, his tone sharpening just slightly.

There it was.

The line.

"I didn't kill him," Ryan said plainly.

Maddie hadn't said he did.

But the fact that he said it anyway, that mattered.

"I didn't think you did," she stammered.

Ryan studied her for a second.

Like he was deciding whether to believe that.

"Good," he said finally.

Then, just as quickly as before, he stepped back.

Conversation over.

Tara let out a breath as they walked away.

"Okay," she said. "So, he's not denying it."

"Not the flirtation," Maddie said. Because he *had* denied murder.

"But he's not spiraling either," Tara added. "Which I feel like I would be if someone accused me of murder before 8 a.m."

Maddie almost smiled, but her mind was elsewhere.

Vanessa didn't trust Derek.

Ryan confronted him.

Anika handled him.

"This is bigger than we thought," Maddie said quietly. "How are we supposed to know what's relevant and what's not?" More a statement than question.

Tara glanced at her. "I have absolutely no clue."

Because now, this wasn't just about Derek showing up.

It was about what led to him showing up.

And what they talked about before she left.

And most importantly, why it mattered enough to act.

CHAPTER 18
WEDNESDAY | ROUTINES

MADDIE MOVED through the morning on autopilot: breakfast, meds, brush teeth, clothes, shoes, backpack, the quiet negotiations that came with getting Lennon out the door without tipping the balance too far in either direction.

Normal.

Everything looked normal.

It wasn't.

Carline filled the way it always did. Same cars. Same rhythm. Same clusters of conversation that Maddie usually avoided.

Today, she didn't.

She watched.

Not the obvious things.

The small ones.

Who stood where. Who talked to who. Who avoided eye contact. Who leaned in.

Patterns.

"You're doing it again," Tara said, appearing beside her.

Maddie didn't look away. "Doing what?"

"Staring like you're about to solve something."

Maddie exhaled. "I'm trying to figure out what we're missing."

Tara followed her gaze.

Maddie finally looked at her. "It's Vanessa."

"What about her?" Tara asked.

Maddie hesitated.

Because she didn't have it fully yet.

Just pieces.

"She wasn't reacting," Maddie said slowly. "Not like everyone else."

Tara frowned. "To Derek?"

"To everything." Maddie leaned back against her car. "Donna said that Vanessa didn't trust him. Chloe said she was careful. Evan said she was distracted by something."

Tara nodded. "Okay…"

Maddie shook her head. "There has to be more to it."

"You think she knew something?"

Maddie didn't answer right away.

Because now, she did.

"I think she was watching for something," Maddie said.

Tara crossed her arms. "Like what?"

"Chloe said something about *what she's been through* but didn't give any details."

"Vague, but probably important."

Maddie's gaze drifted across the line again.

Parents talking.

Kids moving.

The same routine.

And then, it clicked.

"The notebook," Maddie said.

Tara blinked. "What notebook?"

Maddie turned to her. "The green one! She always had it… At carline. In her car. Writing things down."

Tara frowned, thinking. "I thought that was like... schedules or something."

"So did I," Maddie said. "Until she *clearly* wrote something about me." A scoff. "She wasn't just sitting there. She was watching. Tracking."

Tara's expression shifted. "Tracking what?"

Maddie shook her head. "I don't know yet." But she knew one thing. "It wasn't nothing."

The bell rang.

Cars started moving, but Maddie couldn't let it go.

"If she was paying that much attention," Tara said slowly, "then she wrote down anything she deemed important."

Maddie nodded. "Which means..."

"It's somewhere," Tara finished. A shrug.

Silence settled between them.

Because now, this wasn't just a theory.

It was a direction.

They needed that notebook.

"Do you think the police have it?" Tara asked.

Maddie's stomach tightened slightly. "No."

Tara raised an eyebrow. "You sound sure."

Maddie thought about it.

About Greg.

About the footage.

About everything the police had focused on.

"They're looking for Vanessa," she said. "Not what she left behind."

That was the difference.

Tara let out a slow breath. "Okay. So... what are we saying here?"

Maddie looked in the direction of her neighborhood.

In the direction of Vanessa's house.

"I think whatever happened," she said, "clues to it are in that notebook."

A solid ten seconds of silence held.

"And I don't think anyone's found it yet."

Tara followed her gaze. "Or maybe she took it with her?"

"Maybe, but there's only one way to be certain."

Tara didn't respond.

But she didn't disagree.

CHAPTER 19
WEDNESDAY | INSIDE

They didn't talk about it like a plan.

That would have made it real.

IT WAS EVENING, the kids were asleep, and Tara and Maddie were heading out for a walk. Just a little walk around the neighborhood.

"We're just walking," Tara said.

"Right," Maddie replied.

"Just... seeing?"

"Seeing," Maddie echoed.

Neither of them said *breaking in.*

And naturally, the goal was to not *break* anything.

Joon sat at the front door, tail thumping against the floor as soon as Maddie reached for her shoes.

"No," Maddie said immediately.

Joon tilted her head.

"Absolutely not."

The tail kept going.

"We could use her for protection," Tara offered.

"What? Drown them in slobber?"

"Whatever works."

Maddie opened the door just enough to slip through, blocking Joon with her leg. "Stay."

Joon did not stay.

It took thirty full seconds, a treat, and a firm door close before Maddie finally stepped out, slightly out of breath.

Tara was already halfway down the driveway. "You good?" she called.

"Define good."

They wore the finest in cat-burglar chic. At least for a summer day. Black t-shirt, denim shorts, and black sneakers. Tara wore her hair tied back in a low ponytail. The Hardy Boys. All they were missing was a magnifying glass.

They walked.

Not too fast.

Not too slow.

Trying to look like two people who were absolutely not about to make a questionable decision.

They approached Vanessa's house quickly.

Same as before.

Neat. Quiet. Unassuming.

Maddie slowed. "This is a bad idea," she said.

"Yeah," Tara agreed.

Neither of them stopped.

The front yard was still.

No movement. No sound.

Just the faint hum of a neighborhood going about its day.

Maddie's phone buzzed.

Loud.

Sharp.

Obnoxious.

They both froze.

"Turn it off!" Tara hissed. "Turn it off!"

"I thought it *was* off!"

"It's not off!"

"I can tell that!"

Maddie fumbled with her phone, nearly dropping it before finally silencing it.

They stood there for another panicked moment.

Listening.

Waiting.

Nothing.

"Okay," Tara whispered. "Great start."

Maddie exhaled slowly. "Let's just... be quick."

"Quick," Tara agreed.

Maddie remembered the vantage point from Greg's cameras. The cameras were attached to his garage, a clear view of his driveway, the street, and... most of Vanessa's place.

"We can't go through the front," Maddie whispered. "Greg's cameras."

"Back door?" Tara responded

They moved toward the back. On the opposite side of what the cameras could see, through Mark's yard.

Maddie hesitated only a second before reaching for the handle.

Locked.

"There has to be a way in," Maddie muttered. Mostly to herself.

She scanned the area around her and, in lock step, both Tara and Maddie began gently overturning rocks, décor, small flower pots. Maddie noticed a patch of flowers that had been trampled through, a shoe print remaining in the dirt...

"That's odd..." she murmured to herself.

"Got it!" Tara shrieked. Waving a key in the air.

"Shhhhhh….."

With the help of the key, the doorknob turned.

Both of them paused.

"Are we *really* doing this?" Maddie thought aloud and to herself.

"This feels… wrong," Tara whispered.

"Everything about this feels wrong."

Maddie pushed the door open slowly.

The house was quiet.

Not empty.

Just quiet.

They stepped inside.

Carefully.

Like the house might notice them.

Like Vanessa would return and know they had been here.

It smelled clean.

Faintly like laundry detergent.

Nothing stale. Nothing abandoned.

Maddie glanced around.

Living room.

Neat. Minimal.

A throw blanket folded precisely over the arm of the couch. No clutter. No chaos.

"She didn't leave in a panic," Maddie said quietly.

Tara nodded. "Doesn't look like it."

They moved further in.

The kitchen was the same.

Clean counters. A drying rack with a few dishes. A calendar on the wall.

"Do you think she…" Tara started.

"Cleaned before she left?" Maddie finished. "I absolutely do."

Maddie stepped closer.

Everything was labeled.

Like, everything.

Snacks.
Lunch.
After-school.

Her chest tightened slightly.

Vanessa's pantry was a sight to behold. If she wasn't a little creeped out, she'd be jealous.

"Have you seen the movie *Sleeping with the Enemy*?" Tara asked softly.

Maddie laughed at that, recalling the scene in which Julia Roberts returns home discovering her kitchen not in disorder, but order. A telltale sign that her psycho-ex was near.

"It's not quite *that* level," she retorted.

There were no extra shoes by the door.

No toothbrush sitting out by the bathroom sink.

No sign of anyone *really* living there.

Maddie swallowed.

Then forced herself to move.

"Okay," she said quietly. "Notebook."

They split without saying it.

Maddie checked the obvious places first.

Counter.
Drawers.
A stack of mail.
Nothing.

Tara opened a cabinet.

"Why would it be in there?" Maddie whispered.

"I don't know," Tara replied curtly. "I'm just looking."

Another room.

Ellie's.

Maddie paused in the doorway.

Small bed.

Stuffed animals lined neatly along the wall.

A nightlight.

Everything in its place.

Too in its place.

"She planned this," Maddie said.

"Maybe..." Tara didn't argue.

A car passed outside.

Headlights swept briefly across the room.

They fell to the ground, ducking out of sight for fear the shadows would give them away.

"Okay, I hate this," Tara whispered.

"Same."

The light passed.

Silence returned.

Maddie exhaled slowly. "I was not cut out for a life of crime."

Think.

Vanessa was organized.

Intentional.

Everything had a place.

So the notebook wouldn't be random.

It would be...

"Maddie," Tara whispered sharply.

Maddie turned.

Tara stood near the entryway.

Pointing.

"Her car."

Maddie blinked. "What?"

"She always had it in the SUV," Tara said. "You said that."

Maddie's stomach dropped.

Of course.

They moved quickly now.

Still quiet.

But faster.

Back through the house.

Out the door.

The driveway felt too open.

Too exposed.

Maddie tried to think back to what Greg would be able to see on his cameras, and army-crawled from the back gate to the SUV door opposite Greg's house.

Tara couldn't help but chuckle. A low whistle before she whisper-shouted, "Get it, G.I. Jane!"

Maddie glared back.

Her hands trembled slightly as she reached for the SUV door.

Locked.

"Of course it's locked," Tara muttered. It was almost comical.

Tara returned to the house and a moment later emerged with a set of keys. "Saw them in the most organized catch-all drawer I've ever seen," she whispered across the yard to Maddie.

She tossed them her way.

An easy catch.

She unlocked the door.

Slowly.

Carefully.

The interior was just as clean, but she had to move quick.

The dome light glowed.

Greg would definitely know that someone had opened the door.

But if they acted quickly and secretly, he wouldn't know who.

The car was organized. Intentional.

Glove box. Nothing.

Center console. Nothing.

Think.

Not random.

She looked down.

In a slim, zippered pouch tucked neatly between the driver's seat and the cupholders.

Her breath caught. And slowly, she reached for it. Unzipped it. Inside there was a...

Green.

Deep emerald.

Notebook.

Now, this wasn't just a theory.

Maddie held it in her hands, the weight of it heavier than it should have been.

Quietly making her way back to Tara.

"Okay," Tara whispered.

"Okay," Maddie echoed.

They had it.

And whatever was inside...

Was about to change everything.

CHAPTER 20
WEDNESDAY | SIGNALS

BY THE TIME Maddie got home, the notebook was physically weighing on her. Tara left Maddie with a plan to discuss it over U-Brewed the following day. It was nearing 10 o'clock, both were tired, and Tara's sitter was probably about to send out a search party.

The notebook wasn't large. Not bulky. Just a small, emerald green notebook that could have easily been overlooked on a cluttered counter or tucked into the bottom of a bag. But now that it sat in her hands, it carried weight. The kind that settled somewhere behind her ribs and refused to move.

Lennon was still awake.

"He's been requesting you for the last hour," Kent groaned.

"Sorry."

"I tried to get him to bed, no luck. Wanted his mom."

Maddie took over. Kent had thankfully handled meds and dinner, but Lennon needed a bath and to go to sleep. It was way past bedtime, and she didn't dare send him to school tomorrow smelling the way he did after a day of playing in

the heat. The steady rhythm of life altered because Maddie had broken routine.

Maddie moved through it all on autopilot, she placed the notebook safely on the kitchen counter, away from Joon and her frantic tail.

She ran warm water for Lennon's bath, washed his hair, put him in pajamas, and then to bed. As soon as his eyes closed, she returned to the notebook.

She hadn't opened it yet.

Not because she didn't want to.

Because she did.

Too much.

Maddie found herself at the kitchen counter, the house quieter in a way that made everything feel more pronounced.

She opened it.

It was written like a journal with a date on every page and small snippets from the day. As much as Maddie wanted to look inside, she now felt as though it was an invasion of Vanessa's privacy. But she had to know the secrets it held.

She breathed in deeply and flipped to a random page.

February 2nd
Lindsay moved money again today. Savings nearly emptied the same afternoon Derek made that unusually large deposit. Maybe a coincidence. Maybe not. She looked anxious when she came in. More embarrassed than anything.

Maddie frowned slightly, flipping to another page.

December 22nd
Anika and Ryan looked perfect at the holiday

party. Smiling, laughing, coordinated sweaters, all the right answers. But something about it felt practiced. Too careful. Ellie loves their boys. Maybe I should invite them all to the trampoline park over break.

Short entries. Repeated patterns. Names usually, a few initials.

April 12th
Another call tonight. No voice, just breathing. I hung up twice, and they still called back. Maybe it's nothing. Maybe it's him. I'm going to ask for more help tomorrow, either way. Ellie stays safe first. Always.

She reached for her phone without looking away from the notebook.

"Tara," she said as soon as the call connected.

"I was waiting," Tara replied immediately.

Maddie exhaled softly, flipping another page. "Okay, so… this is not what I thought it was."

"That sounds promising."

"It's not organized like evidence," Maddie said. "It's more like… observations. Journal entries almost."

There was a pause on the other end of the line. "About what?"

"People," Maddie said. "Everyone."

She leaned against the counter, scanning the page more carefully now. The entries weren't random thoughts scribbled down in panic. They were measured. Intentional. Vanessa had been paying attention to people the same way other people watched traffic or weather patterns.

Noticing changes.
Behavior.
Tone.
Consistency.

Another thing to note, Vanessa had beautiful handwriting. Of course she did.

"She was watching everyone in carline?" Tara asked.

"Not just carline," Maddie replied quietly. "Life. Conversations. Patterns. She was trying to figure people out."

"For what?"

Maddie frowned slightly. "I honestly think… trust. She was trying to decide if she could trust them."

That shifted the tone immediately.

She turned another page.

The entries weren't accusatory. If anything, some of them felt surprisingly empathetic.

April 15th
Maddie laid on the horn behind me. It would have been comical if she hadn't looked so sad. Most people probably saw impatience. I saw exhaustion. She looks like someone carrying too much by herself. I need to reach out more.

Maddie blinked.

"Okay," Tara said slowly. "That's unexpectedly kind."

I'll make a note to reach out to her more often,

once things calm down. I know she carries more than I can see.

A brief silence settled between them.

"That's actually really sad," Maddie admitted. "Thank goodness I'm in therapy."

"Yeah," Tara said quietly, a hint of a smile in her voice.

Maddie flipped again, specifically looking at the week before she went missing.

April 9th

Lindsay asked about loan options today, but kept insisting she was "just curious." People who are just curious don't wring their hands the entire conversation. Something's wrong financially, and I don't think she wants anyone to know how bad it's getting.

Tara let out a low whistle. "Okay. Bank Vanessa is terrifying."

"She noticed everything," Maddie murmured.

"And apparently judged everyone financially."

Maddie ignored that, already turning to another page.

This entry was different.

Lighter.

Donna means well, but she collects information like it's a competitive sport. Never tell her anything you wouldn't want repeated with concern disguised as sympathy.

Tara barked out a laugh. "OH MY GOD."

"She's not wrong," Maddie said.

"She absolutely isn't."

Maddie smiled despite herself and kept reading.

The notebook shifted again a few pages later, the tone becoming less certain.

More observational.

Tara jokes through almost everything. Humor, sarcasm, volume. It works well enough that people don't ask questions. I can't tell if she's deeply confident or deeply lonely.

Tara went quiet.

Maddie glanced at the phone. "You alive over there?"

"That woman needs to mind her business," Tara muttered.

Maddie laughed softly. "You okay?"

"I don't appreciate being emotionally profiled by a missing banker."

That only made Maddie laugh harder. "That's us, sad and lonely."

Underneath it, something else settled in.

Because Vanessa hadn't been gossiping.

She had been studying people.

Trying to understand them.

Trying to determine who they really were underneath whatever version they showed the world.

Another page caught Maddie's attention.

Found out today he may be getting out earlier than expected. I could barely focus the rest of the afternoon. Every routine I built for Ellie suddenly feels temporary again. Need to update emergency contacts. Need a new plan.

The humor disappeared instantly.

Tara's voice softened. "Who is that about?"

"No clue. Maybe Chloe might know."

Maddie stared at the page a moment longer before turning it carefully.

The next entries became less personal and more fragmented, like Vanessa had started noticing things she didn't fully understand yet.

Derek stayed longer again tonight.
Raised voice.
Too comfortable lately.
Watching everyone else too closely.

Maddie's stomach tightened slightly.

"She was paying attention to him before everything happened," she said quietly.

"Because she didn't trust him?"

"I think because she realized something was off."

She flipped again.

More entries.

Patterns.

Repeated observations.

Same car.
Earlier than usual.
Lights already on.
Off schedule.

Watch closer.

Maddie rubbed lightly at her temple.

"She wasn't paranoid," she said finally. "This is too consistent."

"She was building something," Tara replied.

"Yeah," Maddie agreed. "I think she was trying to understand what kind of people she was surrounded by."

A silence settled between them again, quieter this time.

Not confusion.

Recognition.

Maddie looked back down at the notebook, suddenly understanding why closing it had felt wrong before.

Because this wasn't evidence.

It was perspective.

Vanessa had been quietly collecting pieces of people long before anyone realized something bad was coming.

And somehow, without fully understanding it herself, she had gotten close enough to the truth to become part of it.

CHAPTER 21
THURSDAY | FRICTION

THURSDAY MORNING DIDN'T FEEL the same.

Nothing had actually changed. The line of cars still curved around the building, engines idling, parents half-engaged in conversations they'd had a hundred times before, but Maddie couldn't unsee it now.

Patterns.

That's what Vanessa had been tracking.

And now Maddie was too.

She pulled into the carline slower than usual, eyes moving —not just forward, but outward. Who was early. Who was late. Who was exactly where they always were.

And who wasn't.

Lennon hummed softly beside her, focused on his iPad, blissfully unaware of the shift happening just inches away.

Maddie glanced at the clock.

8:30 on the dot.

She didn't know why that mattered.

Only that it did.

Two cars ahead, Donna stood outside her SUV, already mid-conversation, her voice carrying just enough to make sure it was heard.

Same spot.

Same energy.

Consistent.

Maddie's eyes moved past her.

Lindsay.

In her usual place. Sunglasses on, phone in hand, posture relaxed in a way that felt more intentional than casual. She was exactly the perception she wanted people to have of her.

Also consistent.

Then... Mark.

Maddie's gaze lingered.

He wasn't far off.

Not enough for anyone else to notice.

But enough.

A different position in line. A slight shift in timing. Just... not quite where he should have been.

Maddie felt something tighten in her chest.

She reached over, flipping open the notebook just enough to glance at the page she'd been stuck on the night before.

He's watching me too.

Her fingers stilled.

"Mum," Lennon said from the backseat.

Maddie blinked, looking his direction.

"Nothing, baby," she said, offering a quick smile. "Just thinking."

Drop-off moved quickly.

Too quickly.

Maddie barely registered Lennon climbing out, Miss Merissa's warm greeting, the familiar routine that usually grounded her.

Today, it didn't.

Because now, she was watching.

Ryan Patel stood near the far end of the lot, coffee in hand, posture relaxed in a way that felt practiced rather than natural.

Consistent.

Maddie parked and proceeded to approach before overthinking it.

"Hey," she said.

Ryan glanced up, offering a polite nod. "Morning."

No small talk.

Good.

"We've already talked about Derek," Maddie said. "I'm not going to ask you the same questions again."

Ryan's brow lifted slightly, interest piqued. "Then what are you asking?"

Maddie held his gaze. "Was something off? Before everything happened."

A moment.

Not confusion.

Consideration.

"That depends on what you mean by 'off,'" Ryan said.

"Not personal," Maddie clarified. "I just remember you said Derek did some stuff for your company. "

Ryan shifted his grip on his coffee, eyes flicking briefly past her before returning. He finally said, "There were inconsistencies."

Maddie's stomach tightened. "What kind?"

"Things that didn't line up. Numbers that should've matched and didn't. Timing issues. Reports that came in later than they should have. Reports that looked like they had been modified."

"That sounds like more than a bad week."

"It wasn't a good one," Ryan said evenly.

Maddie studied him. "You think he was messing up?"

Ryan's mouth pressed into something that wasn't quite a

smile. "I think Derek was dealing with more than he was letting on."

Not the same thing.

"He was distracted," Maddie said.

Ryan didn't answer right away.

Which was answer enough.

"More than usual?"

Ryan took a slow sip of his coffee. "Yes."

Maddie shifted slightly. "Distracted by what?"

Ryan looked at her then, really looked at her.

Measured.

"You're asking the wrong question," he said.

Maddie frowned. "Then what's the right one?"

Ryan held her gaze for a second longer. "Who noticed."

That landed.

"People noticed?" Maddie asked.

Ryan shrugged. "People always notice. The question is who pays attention."

Maddie's mind flicked, fast.

Notebook.

Patterns.

Vanessa.

"And you did?" she asked.

Ryan shook his head. "Not my job."

That tracked.

"Did he seem worried?" Maddie asked.

Ryan didn't hesitate. "Yes."

Not defensive.

Not emotional.

Just certain.

Ryan continued, "Derek was always a guy with a plan."

Maddie nodded once. "Okay. That helps."

As she turned to leave, he added, "Whatever you think this is…"

Maddie paused.

"It's probably not small…and it probably doesn't have to do with finances."

She didn't respond.

Didn't need to.

Back at her car, Maddie didn't start the engine right away.

Instead, she sat there, notebook open on the passenger seat, her eyes moving between the page and the parking lot beyond her windshield.

Derek.

Lindsay.

And then...

The notes without names.

Without initials.

Just patterns.

Just behavior.

Her gaze lifted again.

Donna... still talking.

Lindsay... still watching.

Mark... Slightly off.

Maddie exhaled slowly.

Vanessa hadn't been guessing.

She had been paying attention.

Tracking.

Noticing.

And now, Maddie was too.

She closed the notebook, her grip tightening just slightly as she finally started the car.

Because this wasn't just about who had been there.

Or what had happened.

It was about who had seen it coming.

And for the first time, Maddie had a feeling she was getting closer.

CHAPTER 22
THURSDAY | AWARENESS

BY THE TIME Maddie got home, her brain hadn't slowed down. If anything, it had gotten louder.

Ryan's words replayed in the background while she moved through the kitchen on autopilot, setting down her keys, opening the fridge without really looking inside it, and grabbing her 'in case of emergency' bottle of wine.

There were inconsistencies.

You're asking the wrong question.

Who noticed.

That part stayed with her the most.

Not who benefited. Not who fought with Derek. Not even those who hated him enough to want him gone.

Who noticed. Was he implying Vanessa?

Maddie picked the notebook back up from the counter and turned it over once in her hands before opening it again. The pages looked different now than they had the night before. Less chaotic. Less cryptic.

More intentional.

Vanessa hadn't been collecting clues.

She had been studying people.

The front door opened before Maddie heard a knock. A second later came the familiar sound of Tara dropping her bag somewhere it absolutely did not belong.

"Well?" Tara called from the entryway.

"In here," Maddie replied.

Tara walked into the kitchen, sunglasses pushed into her hair despite the fact it was nearly evening. She took one look at Maddie and narrowed her eyes.

Maddie extended a glass of pinot noir her way; she took it with glee.

"You look like you either solved the case or started a second one," Tara said.

"Honestly? Unclear."

Tara slid onto one of the stools by the counter. "Excellent. Love the ambiguity."

Maddie pushed the notebook toward her. "We've been looking at this wrong."

Tara immediately leaned in. "Okay, explain."

"She wasn't making random notes," Maddie said. "She was trying to understand people."

Tara flipped the notebook open, reading a few passages to herself.

"She noticed things most people wouldn't," Maddie said quietly.

Tara turned another page, this time reading out loud.

Donna would survive any apocalypse entirely through networking and unsolicited information. I adore the woman, but she absolutely exhausts me at times.

"She somehow managed to compliment and insult her at the same time." Maddie sighed, raising her glass in support.

"She's not wrong. That woman would absolutely barter with gossip. Honestly, it's impressive."

Maddie moved around the counter and leaned beside Tara, looking down at the pages together now. "That's what I mean. This isn't gossip. She was paying attention to behavior."

Tara kept reading.

Ryan stayed in his truck almost ten minutes after pick-up today before driving away. Looked upset. Didn't want anyone to see it.

The humor faded slightly.

"That feels different," Tara said quietly.

Maddie nodded. "Yeah."

Another page.

Lindsay smiles every time someone talks to her, even when they interrupt her. I don't think she realizes she apologizes for almost everything. I'm going to help her develop a backbone.

Tara frowned slightly. "Okay, now I feel bad for half this town."

Maddie leaned back against the counter, arms folded loosely. "She wasn't judging them. I know some of it comes across harsh, but she was really trying to figure out who people actually were underneath everything."

Tara glanced back down.

Maddie notices everyone else before herself. Behind her at U-Brewed, and she forgot her own drink in the pick-up line again because Lennon was having a difficult time.

Maddie groaned softly. "Okay. I don't love being perceived."

Tara smirked. "No, this is incredible. You're basically a nature documentary to this woman. *Maddie in the Wild.*"

"Please stop talking."

Tara laughed and flipped another page.

Then her expression shifted.

"What?" Maddie asked.

Tara tilted the notebook slightly toward her.

Tara is impossible to get a real read on. Uses humor like body armor. Everyone thinks she's fearless because she says the uncomfortable thing first.

Maddie glanced sideways at her carefully. "They just need more time to get to know you. You grow on people… like a fungus."

"Hardy-har-har," Tara deadpanned, closing the notebook halfway. "Again. Missing banker needs boundaries."

But this time the joke landed softer.

More thoughtful.

Maddie reached over and gently took the notebook back.

"She saw things," Maddie said quietly.

"Too many things," Tara replied.

Maddie flipped farther into the notebook, the tone of the entries slowly changing as she moved deeper. The earlier pages felt observational, even warm at times. But the latter ones felt sharper. More uneasy.

More focused on Derek.

Derek watches conversations instead of participating in them. Like he's trying to figure out what people know.

Another page.

Something changed after the fundraiser. More tension. More calls. More cash moving around.

Tara straightened slightly. "Okay. There it is."

Maddie nodded slowly.

Vanessa had noticed the shift before anyone else admitted there was one. The fundraiser was months ago.

Another entry caught her eye.

Someone called again tonight. No voicemail. Just silence.

The room quieted immediately.

She turned another page.

Need to stop assuming people are harmless just because they're familiar.

That one sat with both of them for a second. Who could that be about?

A knock at the front door interrupted the silence.

Tara looked up immediately. "If that's Donna, I'm hiding."

Maddie was already sliding the notebook into a drawer.

A second later, Tara opened the door, and Maddie poured another glass of wine.

Donna stood there exactly as expected, dressed as if she had somewhere significantly more glamorous to be. "Well," Donna said as she stepped inside without waiting to be invited, "this feels secretive."

"It's not," Tara replied automatically.

Donna smiled like she didn't believe her for a second. "I figured I'd check in." She glanced between them. "Everyone's talking."

"When aren't they?" Maddie said.

"Yes, but now people are pretending it's concern instead of entertainment."

That got a reluctant laugh out of Tara.

Donna wandered farther into the kitchen, lowering her voice slightly. "I heard Derek wasn't just struggling financially."

Maddie straightened. "What do you mean?"

Donna shrugged. "I mean, I heard money was moving around in ways it shouldn't have been."

"How do you know that?" Maddie asked.

Donna gave her a look. "Information has a way of finding me."

"Terrorizing people through gossip is not a personality trait," Tara said.

"It absolutely is." Donna scrunched her face into a knowing smile.

Maddie tried not to react. "Did someone specifically tell you something?"

Donna hesitated just long enough to matter. "Mark mentioned Derek had more going on than people realized."

"What kind of 'more going on'?" Tara asked.

Donna shook her head. "Nothing specific. Just... that

Derek wasn't nearly as put together as he wanted people to think."

Maddie thought about Vanessa quietly collecting observations in her notebook while Mark seemed to do the exact same thing silently in his head.

"You know what's weird?" Tara asked suddenly. "Everyone suddenly has opinions now."

Donna laughed softly. "People always notice things eventually. They just wait until it feels safe to say them out loud."

That landed harder than Maddie expected. Because it felt true.

A few minutes later, Donna drifted back toward the door, clearly satisfied she had contributed something useful.

"Well," she said, downing her last sip of wine, "if you two Nancy Drews solve anything..." Donna smiled and let herself out.

The house fell quiet again once the door shut behind her.

Tara turned back toward Maddie slowly. "Okay. That was not nothing."

"No," Maddie agreed quietly.

She reopened the notebook, slower this time.

The entries about Derek.

The growing unease.

The unnamed observations.

Off schedule.

Earlier than usual.

Watching too closely.

"She was building toward something," Tara said softly.

Maddie nodded. "I think she realized something was wrong before she understood exactly what it was."

"And now?" Tara asked.

Maddie looked back down at the pages.

At the observations.

At the patterns.

At the things Vanessa noticed because she paid attention when everyone else stopped looking.

"I can feel it," Maddie said quietly. "We're close to something."

CHAPTER 23
FRIDAY | FRACTURES

FRIDAY MORNING CAME FASTER than Maddie wanted it to.

Not because she was tired, though she was, but because her brain hadn't really stopped. It had just shifted into something quieter. Sharper. Like it was working in the background, whether she approved of it or not. Replaying what she was told. What she read.

The notebook sat on the passenger seat again.

Open this time.

She didn't even remember opening it.

Carline looked the same, but it didn't feel the same.

Donna: already outside her car, mid-conversation.

Lindsay: same spot, same sunglasses, same stillness.

Mark...

Maddie's eyes caught on him.

Back where he usually stood.

Or close enough.

Which somehow felt worse.

"Okay," she murmured.

"Mum."

Maddie blinked. "Nothing, baby. Love you."

Drop-off passed in a blur.

Routine happened around her while her mind stayed somewhere else entirely.

Because now, she wasn't just watching.

She was comparing.

Lindsay lingered like she always did. That hadn't changed.

But now Maddie noticed something else.

She wasn't scrolling.

She wasn't distracted.

She was... observing.

Maddie walked over. "Hey."

Lindsay lowered her sunglasses just enough to see her. "Maddie. Crazy week, huh?"

"That's one way to put it."

A pause.

Not awkward.

Measured.

"I wanted to ask you something," Maddie said. "And I'm not asking as... you know... gossip."

Lindsay's brow lifted slightly. "Then what are you asking as?"

Maddie didn't hesitate. "As someone who thinks Derek was lying to more than one person."

That landed.

Lindsay studied her for a second longer than necessary. "Okay."

Maddie exhaled slightly. Good. "You invested with him."

"I did."

"You lost money?"

"I did."

No deflection.

No performance.

"How much?" Maddie asked.

Lindsay didn't flinch. "Enough to notice."

"That's not an answer."

"No," Lindsay agreed. "But it's the one I'm giving."

Fair.

"What made you realize something was wrong?" Maddie asked.

Lindsay hesitated. Then... "He stopped being consistent."

Maddie's stomach tightened.

"He used to send reports every Friday," Lindsay continued. "Same time. Same format. Clean. Predictable."

Maddie nodded slowly.

Patterns.

"And then?" she asked.

"They started shifting," Lindsay said. "Different days. Different numbers. Small changes at first."

"How small?"

Lindsay looked at her. "Small enough that if you weren't paying attention, you'd miss it."

That sounded familiar.

"And I did. Miss it. For a while at least."

Maddie leaned slightly against the car beside her. "What kind of changes?" she asked.

Lindsay let out a breath. "Transfers that didn't match the reports. Accounts that looked right on paper but... weren't matching up when I looked at the accounts online."

Maddie's pulse ticked up. "Like money was being moved?"

Lindsay met her gaze. "Yes. Maybe."

That wasn't speculation.

That was something.

"Did you confront him?" Maddie asked.

"I tried," Lindsay said. "He always had an explanation."

"And you believed him?"

"For longer than I should have."

A beat.

"What made you stop?" Maddie asked.

Lindsay's jaw shifted slightly. "He slipped."

Maddie stilled. "How?"

"He referenced an account I'd never seen before. Not in any report. Not in any summary."

"That's not a small mistake."

"No," Lindsay said quietly. "It's not."

Maddie's mind moved fast now. "You think he was doing this to other people?"

"I know he was."

That widened everything.

"Did anyone else catch on?" Maddie asked.

Lindsay hesitated. "Someone did."

Maddie's breath caught slightly. "Who?"

Lindsay didn't answer right away. Instead, she glanced across the lot, and Maddie followed her gaze.

Mark.

He wasn't looking at them, but his posture had shifted. Just slightly.

Maddie turned back. "Did you tell him?"

Lindsay shook her head. "No. But he asked questions."

That wasn't nothing.

"What kind of questions?" Maddie pressed.

"The kind where you realize someone else is noticing the same things you are."

Maddie felt something click. Not fully, but enough. "And Vanessa?"

This time, Lindsay didn't hesitate. "She knew."

The words landed clean.

"How do you know that?" Maddie asked.

Lindsay held her gaze.

"Because she stopped pretending she didn't," Lindsay

said sternly. "That woman worked at our bank; I'm sure she has a very clear picture of everyone in this town's finances. Mine, Derek's, yours."

That wasn't dramatic. It was certain.

Maddie's grip tightened on her keys. "She said something to you?"

"No. But she didn't have to. I could see that she was watching him. Not casually. Intentionally."

"And after that?"

Lindsay slid her sunglasses back into place. "Things escalated."

Not explained.
Not detailed.
But clear.

"For what it's worth," she added, "whatever happened that night…" She paused. "It didn't start there. This was about more than money."

Maddie nodded slowly. "Yeah. I know."

As Lindsay walked away, Maddie didn't move.

Because this, this wasn't a theory anymore.

Derek wasn't just sloppy.

He wasn't just inappropriate.

He was stealing.

From multiple people.

And Vanessa had figured it out.

CHAPTER 24

FRIDAY | ALIGNMENT

WHEN MADDIE GOT HOME after drop-off, the noise in her head had started organizing itself into something quieter. Not gone exactly, but clearer.

Ryan's comments from earlier in the week kept replaying in fragments while she moved through the house.

Derek wasn't just careless.
He was hiding something.
And Vanessa had known it.

Tara was already there when Maddie walked in. Of course she was. Her shoes sat abandoned near the front door, one tipped onto its side, as if she had kicked them off mid-thought. A half-finished coffee rested beside her phone on the counter, and the television hummed quietly in the background even though Tara clearly wasn't watching it.

Tara looked up immediately when Maddie entered the kitchen. "Well?"

Maddie dropped her keys onto the counter and slid the notebook toward her. "He was stealing."

Tara straightened instantly. "Okay," she said slowly. "That feels like a pretty major development."

"It is," Maddie replied as she leaned back against the counter. "Lindsay confirmed it. Accounts weren't matching up, deposits were showing up where they shouldn't have, and money was moving around without documentation. Derek wasn't just bad at his job. He was actively covering things."

Tara stared at her for a second before glancing back down at the notebook. "So this wasn't incompetence."

"No," Maddie said quietly. "It was intentional."

That changed the feeling in the room immediately.

Tara reached for the notebook again, flipping it open much more carefully this time. Her eyes scanned across the pages, slowing as she read instead of skimming.

"She knew," Tara murmured.

"I think she knew pieces of it," Maddie clarified. "Not everything. But enough to realize something was wrong."

Tara paused on one entry and read it aloud. "'Lindsay moved money again today. Savings nearly emptied the same afternoon Derek made an unusually large deposit.'" She looked up. "That's not a random observation."

"No," Maddie agreed. "That's someone who worked at the bank, noticing inconsistencies."

Tara nodded slowly, her expression sharpening as she turned another page. "'Derek watches conversations instead of participating in them lately. Like he's trying to figure out what people know.' She was watching him."

Maddie shook her head slightly. "Not just him. Everyone."

That was the part finally starting to make sense.

Vanessa hadn't been keeping a list of suspects. She had been quietly studying the people around her, trying to figure out who they actually were beneath whatever version they showed everyone else.

Maddie moved beside Tara and pointed toward another section of the notebook. "Look at these."

Tara frowned slightly as she scanned the entries.

Same car.
Earlier than usual.
Lights already on.
Watching too closely.
Off schedule again.

"These don't have names," Tara noticed.

"Exactly."

Several entries included initials or full names, but others were intentionally vague. No identifiers. Just observations.

Tara looked back up at Maddie. "Why leave names out?"

Maddie had spent most of the drive home asking herself the same thing. "I honestly don't know," she admitted. "Maybe she wasn't sure yet. Maybe she was protecting someone." She hesitated briefly before adding, "Or protecting herself."

That possibility settled more heavily between them.

Because names made things real.

And real things became dangerous.

Tara closed the notebook halfway and leaned back against the counter. "So we've been treating this like everything started the night Derek showed up at her house."

"But it didn't," Maddie said immediately. She grabbed a scrap of paper and a pen from the drawer beside her, then started writing while she talked. "This started before that night. Maybe days before. Maybe weeks."

Tara stepped closer, watching her write out the timeline. "Walk me through it."

Maddie nodded and tapped the paper with the pen.

"Monday. Derek arrives at Vanessa's house. Evan shows up later. Evan leaves around seven."

"Derek stays," Tara added.

"Right," Maddie said. "And before all of that, Vanessa was already documenting behavior changes. She already knew something was off."

Tara looked back down at the notebook thoughtfully. "So she wasn't reacting," she said slowly. "She was preparing."

"Exactly." Maddie tapped the pen lightly against the counter while her thoughts continued falling into place. "She worked at the bank. She had access to information that other people didn't. Deposits, withdrawals, loans, financial stress. And on top of that, she was paying attention to how people behaved when they were nervous or hiding something."

"She noticed things before everyone else did," Tara said quietly.

"Yeah."

The kitchen fell quiet for a moment.

Maddie flipped farther into the notebook, stopping on one of the later entries. "'Watching everyone else too closely lately.'"

Tara frowned. "That's Derek?"

"I think so."

"And she was getting nervous."

Maddie nodded slowly. "The closer it gets to the night he dies, the more unsettled her entries become."

Tara folded her arms loosely. "Because she realized he was involved in something?"

"Or because she realized he was paying attention to her," Maddie said softly.

That shifted the conversation again.

Neither of them spoke for a second.

Then Tara glanced back toward the unnamed entries. "You still think one of these could be Mark?"

Maddie hesitated before answering. "I think Mark notices

people the same way Vanessa did," she admitted carefully. "The difference is he doesn't write any of it down."

Tara considered that.

"Donna said he mentioned Derek had more going on than people realized," Maddie continued. "Lindsay said he'd been asking questions. And he was one of the first people outside the house that night."

"I mean..." Tara shrugged slightly. "He does live next door."

"I know."

"And being observant doesn't make someone a killer."

"No," Maddie agreed quietly. "But it doesn't remove him either."

That sat between them while Maddie looked back down at the timeline she had written.

Monday.

Derek arrives.

Evan leaves.

Derek stays.

Something happens.

Vanessa runs.

"There's still a gap," Maddie said softly.

Tara stepped closer to the paper. "Where?"

"Between Derek arriving and Vanessa leaving. We know what the cameras showed outside the house, but we still don't know what happened inside."

The silence that followed felt heavier this time.

Because that was it.

That was the missing piece.

"That's where everything is," Tara said quietly.

Maddie nodded slowly. "And probably the only people who know exactly what happened in there..."

She let the sentence trail off.

She didn't need to finish it.

Vanessa.

And someone else.

Maddie looked back down at the notebook, suddenly understanding why the unnamed entries bothered her so much.

Not because they were vague.

Because they were intentional.

Vanessa had chosen who to identify directly.

And who not to.

Finally, Maddie closed the notebook and exhaled slowly. "We need to stop listening to what people are saying."

Tara raised an eyebrow. "Okay..."

Maddie looked back down at the pages one last time. "And start paying attention to what they're doing."

A small smile pulled at Tara's mouth. "You're becoming a little terrifying."

Maddie gave a tired shrug. "Yeah," she admitted quietly.

But for the first time since this all started, it no longer felt like random guessing.

It felt like they were finally getting close.

CHAPTER 25
SATURDAY | SERVICE

SATURDAY FELT different before it even started.

Not quieter. Not calmer. Just heavier.

Maddie stood in front of her closet longer than necessary, staring at clothes that all felt slightly wrong for the occasion. Too casual. Too bright. Too much like a normal day.

Behind her, Joon shifted on the bed with a low huff, settling back into the blankets like none of this applied to her.

Kent leaned against the doorway, already dressed for the day, watching her with a small, patient expression. "It's a funeral," he said gently. "Not a job interview."

"I know," Maddie replied, pulling out a black top and holding it up like she needed confirmation. "It just feels weird."

"It is weird," he said. "You barely knew him, yet you saw him every day."

Maddie hesitated. "That's not really true."

Kent raised an eyebrow. "You talked in carline."

"I watched him in carline," she corrected. "There's a difference."

Kent studied her for a second longer than usual, like he wanted to ask something else, but didn't. "You going alone?"

"Tara's meeting me there. And you're with Lennon. Don't forget, his therapy group starts at 9."

Kent nodded. "We'll be fine."

Maddie gave a small smile, then turned back to the closet. "I know."

Although "fine" felt like a stretch.

Maddie picked out a simple black dress and heels, then shuffled out of the house, doing her best to avoid Joon and her shedding.

The service was held at a small chapel just off the main road, the kind of place Maddie had driven past dozens of times without really noticing. Today, the parking lot was full.

Of course it was.

Small town.

Everyone showed up.

Maddie spotted Tara immediately, leaning against her car, sunglasses on despite the overcast sky.

"You look like a spy," Maddie said as she approached Tara. "I thought we were pretending to be normal today."

Tara shrugged. "We can multitask."

They walked in together, the low hum of conversation wrapping around them as soon as the doors opened.

Soft voices. Measured tones. The kind of quiet that wasn't actually quiet at all.

Maddie's eyes adjusted slowly, scanning without making it obvious.

Donna was near the front, of course. Dressed perfectly, already mid-conversation, her expression arranged into something appropriately somber. Her husband beside her.

Lindsay sat a few rows back, alone, posture straight, hands folded in her lap like she was holding herself together by sheer will.

Ryan stood off to the side, speaking quietly with someone Maddie didn't recognize, his expression controlled, unreadable. Anika must be home with the boys.

Nope, she was sitting in a pew - AJ on one side, Michael on the other.

And then Mark.

Near the back. Standing within the "standing room only" group.

Not hiding. Not exactly blending in either. Just there.

Tara leaned in slightly. "Everyone's here," she murmured. "Even a few of Sara's classmates."

There was one unremarkable absence... Chloe.

They took seats along the side, not too close, not too far. Close enough to observe.

As Maddie settled into her seat, her eyes drifted toward the front row.

Sara sat between two women, her feet not quite touching the floor, her hands folded tightly in her lap, as if she had been told exactly how to sit and was determined to do it right. Her mom sat beside her, one hand resting lightly on her shoulder, fingers curled just enough to keep contact.

Maddie felt that familiar shift in her chest.

They knew that family. Not well, not deeply, but enough. Carline smiles. Quick conversations. School events. The kind of familiarity that comes from seeing someone almost every day without ever really stepping into their life.

And now this.

Sara's eyes stayed forward, wide and unfocused in a way that didn't look like she was listening to anything being said. She looked smaller somehow. Quieter.

"This is too much for a ten-year-old to go through," Maddie said under her breath. Maddie had lost her father when she was in her twenties to a heart attack. It was completely out of the blue, and she doesn't remember keeping it together half as well as Sara was.

Tara nodded, her voice softer than usual. "I can't imagine."

Maddie swallowed, her gaze lingering a second longer.

Sara. It wasn't just a name. It was a child who went to the same school, walked the same halls, and sat in the same carline as Lennon. Sara was a kid who would go back to school on Monday without a dad.

Maddie looked down briefly, pressing her lips together.

For a moment, the notebook, the patterns, the questions, all of it, felt smaller. Not unimportant. Just not the whole picture.

The service started simply. A few words from the officiant. Carefully chosen language about loss, about community, about remembering someone as more than the worst thing that happened to them.

Maddie listened, but not really. Her attention kept drifting. Not to the front. To the room as a whole.

Lindsay didn't cry. She didn't fidget or shift or look uncomfortable. She just sat there, still and composed, like she had already processed whatever she needed to process.

Ryan checked his watch once. Subtle. Quick. But Maddie saw it.

Donna leaned toward someone beside her, whispering something that earned a small, inappropriate smile in return.

And Mark.

Maddie's gaze lingered.

He wasn't watching the service. Not really. His eyes moved the way hers had started to. Tracking. Noticing.

Maddie felt something tighten low in her chest.

"You see that?" Tara whispered.

Maddie didn't look at her. "Yeah."

Because once you started noticing behaviors and patterns, you couldn't stop.

The service ended the way they always did. A soft closing. People standing. Chairs shifting. Conversations started again almost immediately, the heaviness lifting just enough to make space for curiosity.

Maddie stood with Tara, letting the crowd move around them instead of through them.

"Okay," Tara said under her breath. "That was deeply uncomfortable."

"Mmm-hmm," Maddie agreed. "I hate funerals."

People began to gather in small clusters. Donna moved easily between conversations, already collecting information as if it were second nature. They'd have to talk to her again and see if she'd learned anything.

Ryan, along with Anika and the boys, slipped out quickly, barely stopping to speak to anyone. Lindsay stayed seated for a moment longer before finally standing, smoothing her hands over her dress in a small, controlled motion.

Mark didn't move.

Maddie noticed that immediately.

Everyone else shifted. Adjusted. Left or engaged.

Mark stayed exactly where he was, scanning the room.

"That's not normal," Tara said quietly.

"No," Maddie replied. "It's not."

"He's... strange sometimes."

They didn't approach him.

Not yet.

Instead, Lindsay approached them. "That was a lovely service."

Her tone was neutral. Careful.

Maddie nodded. "Yeah."

A beat passed.

"You came," Lindsay said.

It wasn't a question.

"Small town," Tara said lightly. "We show up."

Lindsay's mouth curved slightly. Not quite a smile.

"You holding up okay?" Maddie asked.

Lindsay met her gaze. "I feel terrible for Sara and her mom, but I'm not surprised."

That wasn't the same as okay.

Maddie felt that settle.

"You thought this was going to happen?" Tara asked before Maddie could stop her.

Lindsay's eyes flicked to her, then back to Maddie. "I think," she said slowly, "that people don't get into situations like that overnight. And more often than not, they get what they deserve."

The intensity with which she made that statement shocked Maddie. Did she think Derek deserved this?

"That sounded harsh, didn't it?" Lindsay responded to herself. "I just meant that he wasn't a very good person."

Another beat passed, and Lindsay glanced past them.

Maddie followed her gaze.

Mark.

Still in the same spot. Still watching.

Lindsay's voice dropped slightly. "Gotta be careful who you trust."

That landed heavier than anything else she had said.

Then she stepped away.

Tara let out a quiet breath. "Okay, I officially don't like that."

"Yeah," Maddie said.

Her eyes moved back to Mark.

This time, he was looking directly at her.

Not long. Not obvious.

But enough.

Maddie didn't look away.

For a second, neither of them did.

Then someone stepped between them, breaking the line of sight.

When Maddie looked back, he had moved.

"Did he just leave?" Tara asked as they stepped outside.

Maddie was already scanning the parking lot, keys in hand. "I think so."

Mark's truck pulled out, slow and steady, like he had nowhere urgent to be.

Maddie didn't hesitate.

She started walking.

Tara stared at her for half a second before following. "We are not doing this," she hissed, quickening her pace. "We are absolutely not the kind of people who follow someone after a funeral."

Maddie kept moving. "We're just going the same direction."

"Not comforting."

They slid into Maddie's car just as Mark turned out of the lot. His "If you can read this, you're too close" bumper sticker fading slowly out of view.

Maddie started the engine, easing out behind him.

Not too close. Not too far. Just enough.

Tara gripped the handle above the door. "You realize if he turns and makes eye contact, I'm immediately telling him it was all your idea, and you forced me to come."

"I'm not forcing you to do anything," Maddie said, eyes fixed ahead. "But be honest, this is a little fun, isn't it?"

"I'm not kidding, if we're caught, I will fold instantly," Tara replied. "I was not built for crime."

"We're not the criminals... We're the good guys."

Mark didn't head toward the flower shop. He didn't head home either.

Instead, he turned into a strip mall on the edge of town.

Maddie drove past, trying to look casual, then looped into a lot across the street.

"Was that subtle?" Maddie asked.

"Extremely," Tara said. "I'm impressed."

They watched from a distance.

Mark parked.

And then nothing.

He didn't get out. He didn't move. He just sat there.

Minutes passed.

Tara shifted in her seat. "Maybe he's just sitting? Doom-scrolling?"

"No, people don't just sit like that, in random parking lots," Maddie said. "He's waiting for something."

Right on cue, Mark reached for his phone. He glanced around first. Not casually. Carefully. Then he made a call.

Maddie leaned forward slightly, her attention sharpening.

His posture changed. Tighter. More controlled. Not relaxed. Not normal.

"This is not nothing," Tara said quietly.

"No," Maddie agreed.

Her eyes stayed locked on him.

Because whatever this was, it wasn't part of the story he'd been telling.

CHAPTER 26
SATURDAY | FOLLOW

THEY DIDN'T PLAN on following at first, but they couldn't help themselves.

Maddie kept just enough distance to avoid being obvious, but not enough to lose him, her hands locked at ten and two like that might somehow make the whole thing feel more controlled. Tara had gone quieter beside her, which was never a reassuring sign. When Tara stopped making jokes, it usually meant she was actually nervous.

Mark drove another few blocks before pulling off the main road and into a residential area Maddie didn't recognize. It wasn't their neighborhood, and it wasn't anywhere they had a reason to be.

He parked near the curb beneath a large oak tree, killed the engine, and got out.

Maddie kept driving.

She didn't slow too much. She didn't crane her neck. She just kept going until they reached the corner, then turned.

"Okay," Tara said, exhaling all at once. "Now what?"

Maddie's pulse was thudding harder now. "We go around."

"We should not go around."

"We're already here."

"That is not a legal defense."

Maddie turned onto the next street, looped the block, and came back slower this time. She found a spot two houses down and parked in partial shade, her view not perfect but good enough.

Mark wasn't at a front door.

He wasn't walking up a path, or knocking, or waiting for someone to answer.

He was standing at a mailbox.

Not his.

Not anyone Maddie knew.

He looked around once, quickly and in control, then opened it.

Tara sat up straighter. "Is that..."

"A package," Maddie said quietly as Mark gently placed a small brown package into the compartment.

Maddie felt something cold settle low in her stomach.

"That's not normal," Tara whispered.

"No," Maddie agreed. "It's not."

They stayed where they were, watching him cross back to his truck with that same measured calm. Nothing rushed. Nothing careless. He moved like someone who had practiced looking ordinary.

He got back in and pulled away from the curb.

This time, Maddie didn't start the car.

She just sat there.

Tara turned toward her slowly. "Okay. So now what are we calling this?"

Maddie didn't answer right away.

Because she didn't know.

A payoff? A drop? Money? Information? Something worse?

But whatever it was, it had weight.

"Not florist behavior," Maddie said finally.

That pulled a short, strained laugh out of Tara. "Yeah. I'm gonna go ahead and agree with that."

Maddie looked back toward the empty stretch of road where his truck had disappeared.

Vanessa tracked patterns. Derek moved money. And now Mark was depositing packages in random mailboxes.

The pieces weren't lined up yet, but they were getting closer.

And for the first time, Maddie didn't feel like they were chasing a theory.

She felt like they had just seen part of the cover-up still in motion.

CHAPTER 27
SUNDAY | REALIZATION

MADDIE DIDN'T REALIZE how quiet the house was until the door clicked shut behind her.

Not the kind of quiet that felt calm or earned. The kind that settled in too quickly, pressing in around her, leaving space for thoughts she wasn't sure she wanted to follow all the way through.

She dropped her keys onto the counter and stood there for a second, staring at nothing in particular. The image of Mark at that mailbox kept replaying in her head. The package. The way he looked around first. The way he delivered it, like it was just another errand.

It should have felt like progress.

Instead, it made everything feel more dangerous.

Because if Mark was still doing things like that now, after the police, after the funeral, after all of it, then he wasn't scared enough.

And that meant either he felt protected or that he had no other choice.

Maddie exhaled slowly and pressed her palms into the counter. "Okay," she muttered. "So now what?"

Her phone buzzed against the granite.

Tara.

Of course.

Maddie picked it up immediately. "Hey..."

"I'm still thinking about the mailbox," Tara said.

Maddie blinked. "Okay, good. Same."

"Because that was insane."

"It was."

There was a brief silence, both of them working through the same thought from opposite kitchens.

"So," Tara said, her tone shifting, "if Mark is doing weird secret-mailbox stuff, what exactly does that mean?"

Maddie reached for the notebook without thinking, pulling it from where she'd tucked it out of sight. The green cover felt heavier than it should have. She flipped it open and started scanning again, faster this time.

"I think we've been looking at this wrong," she said.

"How so?"

"We keep looking at one person at a time. Like each person has their own separate issue. Derek and the money. Ryan and Anika. Lindsay and the accounts."

"Okay..."

"But what if this is less about individuals and more about what they know about each other?"

The line went quiet.

"Like leverage?" Tara asked.

"Exactly."

Maddie turned another page.

Vanessa hadn't just been observing people. She had been cataloging them. Patterns. Behaviors. Deviations. Who was where they should be and who wasn't. What time people showed up. What changed.

"Lindsay has money stuff in here," Maddie said. "Ryan has inconsistency stuff. You have... personality notes."

"Still rude."

Maddie ignored that. "Everyone has something," she said quietly. "Everyone except..."

"Who?" Tara asked.

"Mark."

There was a pause.

"What about him?"

Maddie frowned and flipped backward, checking again. "There's almost nothing. Routine observations. Surface stuff. Nothing like what she wrote about everyone else."

"That doesn't make sense," Tara said. "Vanessa noticed everything."

"Exactly."

Maddie's stomach tightened.

Either Vanessa trusted Mark implicitly, or she knew something she didn't trust herself to write down.

And that felt worse.

She thought back to the footage. Derek arriving. The shadow near the side of the house. The missing gap in the timeline. Mark watching people at the funeral instead of mourning. The package left in the mailbox.

Then it clicked just enough to make her stand up straighter.

"We need to go see Greg," she said.

"What for?"

"The footage. I watched for Vanessa and Derek. I need to look for more... We need to look for more."

A sigh came through the phone. "I hate when you get that tone."

"Too bad."

Greg opened the door before Maddie even had a chance to knock.

Again.

"You're back, and you brought a friend," he said, a hint of excitement. Greg clearly knew he was an integral part of Maddie's investigation, and he was enjoying every second of it.

"This is Tara. We have a question," Maddie said.

He gave her a look. "Just one?"

An innocent smile.

He stepped aside anyway, letting them both in.

The same laptop waited on the coffee table. Same setup. Same grainy footage that had already changed shape once in Maddie's mind. This time she didn't sit right away. She hovered, arms crossed loosely, her attention already narrowed.

"I need to watch it slower," she said. "And I need to stop looking at Derek."

Greg studied her for a second, then nodded and restarted the footage.

The timestamp blinked to life.

6:02 p.m.

Derek's car pulled into frame.

Maddie watched differently now. Not the arrival itself. Not the obvious movement. Her eyes moved to the margins of the screen. The edges. The spaces near the side yard and the shadows where someone could disappear without fully disappearing.

"Go back," Tara said.

Greg rewound a few seconds.

"There." Tara pointed to the top corner of the screen.

Greg squinted. "I'm not seeing..."

"A shadow," Maddie said, leaning closer. "I see it. Near the side of the house."

Greg paused the frame and zoomed in as much as he could. The image blurred, stretched, pixelated. But the shape was still there. Faint. Easy to dismiss. Harder to ignore once you've seen it.

A shift.

Movement that didn't belong. 8:14.

"Could be nothing," Greg said, though he didn't sound convinced.

"Or someone who didn't want to be seen," Maddie said.

He didn't argue.

The footage rolled forward again.

Only now it didn't feel empty.

It felt occupied.

Maddie leaned back slowly, the realization settling hard this time.

"Maybe someone else was there," Tara suggested.

Greg frowned. "You think so?"

"I think you're right," Maddie paced, thinking. "I don't think Derek was the only one who showed up that night. Remember the trampled flowers in the back yard when..." She corrected herself, "I remember seeing some flowers that had been stepped on when I was in the back yard. Right between Vanessa's house and the neighbors."

"That could definitely be related," Greg responded. "Vanessa maintains a meticulous yard, and we don't see anyone else come through the front door."

"So now we're thinking someone else was with Vanessa and Derek?" Tara questioned.

"Someone that didn't want to be seen," Maddie confirmed. And now, saying it out loud, it didn't sound like a theory.

It sounded like a missing piece.

Outside, the air felt thicker than before.

Maddie stood on Greg's porch for a second longer than necessary, her mind moving too fast to settle. The funeral. The mailbox. The notebook. The shadow. Mark.

Nothing had clicked fully into place yet.

But the shape of it was there.

And for the first time, Maddie felt something sharper than curiosity.

Not excitement.

Not even fear exactly.

Urgency.

Because if Mark had been there that night, and if he was still cleaning up pieces now, then this wasn't just about understanding what happened.

It was about how long he could keep it buried.

CHAPTER 28
MONDAY | CONVERGENCE

BY MONDAY MORNING, Maddie was running on almost no sleep and far too much certainty.

Not certainty in the way she could prove anything. Not the kind that would hold up in a police report or even survive a direct question from someone smarter than she was. But enough certainty to make the carline feel smaller when she pulled into it. Enough to make every familiar face feel sharper around the edges.

The routine unfolded the way it always did. Cars rolled forward. Doors opened. Teachers waved. Donna was already outside her SUV, talking like she had been waiting all weekend to resume control of the narrative. But Maddie barely registered any of it. Her focus narrowed almost immediately.

Mark was there.

From the backseat, Lennon hummed softly, tapping the window in a rhythm that probably meant he was regulating himself.

Maddie glanced at him in the mirror and smiled automatically. "Almost there, buddy."

He didn't answer. He just kept humming.

Maddie looked back toward the line and found Mark again.

He was talking to another dad now, a fifth grader's dad, she thought. Casual enough from a distance. Nothing anyone else would think twice about. But Maddie had seen him at the funeral. She had seen him at the strip mall. She had seen him at that mailbox.

And now it was impossible to look at him the same way.

Tara launched herself into Maddie's passenger seat the second Piper was out of her car, and Maddie slid into a parking spot.

"You look insane," Tara said. "Your eyes are all big and crazy."

Maddie didn't take her eyes off the carline. "Rude."

"Accurate."

A quiet second passed.

"Did you sleep at all?" Tara asked.

"Not enough. My brain was doing cartwheels."

"Same."

Maddie let out a slow breath. "I keep replaying it."

"The mailbox or the footage?"

"Both."

That got a tired huff of laughter from Tara.

Because that was the problem now. It wasn't one thing. It was all of it. The package. The shadow near the side of the house. The timeline gap. The notes Vanessa hadn't written. The notes she had. Mark's calm. His watching. His certainty.

It all felt connected now.

They just needed to figure out how.

After drop-off, Maddie didn't go straight home. She didn't really decide not to. She just found herself turning into U-Brewed with Tara already following behind her in her own car, like they had both silently agreed this conversation couldn't happen in passing.

They grabbed drinks and took the small table near the

back, the one half-hidden by a fake plant and a chalkboard sign advertising a lavender cold foam special no one in town had asked for.

Maddie slid the notebook onto the table between them.

"Okay," Tara said, wrapping both hands around her cup. "Walk me through your spiraling."

Maddie opened the notebook and turned it toward her. "I don't think the missing information on Mark is accidental."

Tara frowned. "You think Vanessa left it out on purpose?"

"I think Vanessa trusted Mark. They lived next door to each other for years."

"And he was what? Looking out for her?"

"If he was looking out for her, it would explain why he was there. It would explain why Vanessa left the way she did. It would explain why Mark knew enough to keep pointing people in muted directions."

"Everyone keeps saying she ran. But what if she didn't run? What if she left because someone told her she had to?"

The thought landed hard enough that Maddie didn't answer right away.

Because that felt closer to the truth than anything they'd said so far.

Vanessa leaving in the middle of the night with Ellie, bags packed, not frantic but not normal either. The way Chloe said everything she did was about Ellie. The way Evan said she had paid him in advance, like she had expected not to be there.

"She was preparing," Maddie said quietly.

Tara looked back at the notebook. "And then Derek shows up."

"And whatever happened inside that house… It changed everything."

They both went quiet.

Around them, the coffee shop continued as normal. A blender roared somewhere behind the counter. A chair scraped against the floor. Someone laughed too loudly near the front. All ordinary sounds, all somehow irritating now.

Tara broke the silence first. "So what do we do?"

That was the question.

Maddie looked down at the notebook again, then thought of the mailbox. The package. The way Mark had moved like someone delivering something important.

"We need to know what he's hiding," she said. "What if the package wasn't random? What if it was connected to Derek somehow?"

Tara slowly straightened. "Or Vanessa?"

"Cash. Records. Or something he didn't want in his house."

Tara let out a breath through her nose. "Okay, so what? We camp out by random mailboxes now?"

"No," Maddie said. Then, after a beat, "Maybe?"

Tara stared at her. "Maddie."

"I'm kidding."

"You're not."

Maddie wasn't.

But she also didn't know how else to get ahead of someone who was still moving pieces around while everyone else acted like the story had already settled.

She wondered where the police were in their investigation.

Her phone buzzed on the table.

Both of them looked down.

Unknown number.

Maddie frowned and opened it.

Unknown Number
Stop digging.

That was it.

No name. No context. Not exactly a threat, more of a command.

Tara watched her face change. "What?"

Maddie turned the phone around.

Tara read it once, then again. "Well," she said finally, her voice much quieter now. "That feels bad."

Maddie's grip tightened around the edge of the table.

Because this was the shift.

Up until now, they had been the ones watching.

Now someone was watching back.

CHAPTER 29
MONDAY | WATCHED

MADDIE DIDN'T TELL Kent about the text.

Not right away.

She told herself it was because she didn't want to alarm him over something stupid. A prank. A wrong number. Someone in town being dramatic because drama was easier than minding their own business.

But that wasn't the real reason.

The real reason was that once she told him... he would ask her to stop. Stop when she was just starting to feel alive.

So she tucked the phone face down on the counter and moved through the rest of the day on a kind of strained autopilot.

Pick-up. OT. Meds. Dinner. Lennon melting down over the wrong cup and then recovering as if nothing had happened. Kent talking about a podcast episode ad nauseam that she had zero interest in. Joon pacing hopefully every time someone moved in the direction of the kitchen.

The normalcy of it all felt almost insulting.

Because underneath it, Maddie was wound so tightly she could barely think straight.

She waited until Lennon was asleep and Kent was upstairs before texting Tara.

Maddie
You still awake?

The three dots appeared almost instantly.

Tara
Unfortunately, yes.

Maddie grabbed the notebook, her phone, and her drink and stepped out onto the back patio. The air had cooled just enough to make the evening tolerable. The neighborhood was quiet in that deceptive way suburbs always were. Porch lights on. TVs glowing behind curtains. People inside their houses pretending other people's lives weren't any of their business.

Tara answered on the second ring. "I still hate the text," she said instead of hello.

"Same."

"You tell Kent?"

"No."

"Are you going to?"

Maddie looked out into the dark yard. "Not yet."

A pause.

Then Tara said, "So what are we doing?"

Maddie almost laughed.

Not because it was funny. Because, of course, that was the question. Not *should we stop*, not *should we tell someone*, just *what are we doing?*

She looked down at the notebook in her lap and flipped it open again. "I think we go back to the money."

"Okay…"

"Everything keeps leading back to there. Lindsay. Ryan.

The gossip at the funeral. Donna saying Mark knew Derek had more going on than people realized."

"And the package," Tara added.

"And the package."

Maddie rubbed at her forehead. "If Derek was stealing from people, and Vanessa figured it out, then Mark had two reasons to be involved. He was angry, and he knew enough to understand what Derek was really doing."

Tara let that sit. "Crime of passion?"

Maddie didn't respond immediately.

Because she had been circling that exact thought for hours and hated how cleanly it fit.

Not premeditated. Not some elaborate murder plot. A confrontation. An argument. Derek pushing too far with the wrong person. Someone snapped.

Then, Vanessa helping him after? Maybe. Not because she was guilty. Because she was trapped.

They were speculating. Something Mark would have advised them against.

Maddie stared out into the dark. "Chloe said everything Vanessa did was about Ellie."

"Yeah."

"And Evan said she paid him in advance like she knew she'd be gone."

Tara's voice lowered. "You think Mark convinced her to leave."

Maddie swallowed. "I think," she said slowly, "if Derek was threatening her, and then Derek ended up dead, and Mark was standing there telling her it wasn't safe..." She stopped and tried again. "I think she might have believed leaving was the only way to protect Ellie."

The silence on the other end told her Tara was there, too.

It was ugly.

Messy.

But real.

And worse than that, it made emotional sense.

Tara finally spoke. "So what now?"

Maddie looked down at the notebook again, then at the text still sitting on her phone.

Unknown Number
Stop digging.

That meant they were close.

Or it meant they were irritating someone who wanted them scared enough to back off.

Either way, it meant movement.

"We need something concrete," Maddie stated excitedly.

"Such as?"

Maddie thought about the mailbox. About Mark delivering something to be retrieved by someone. But who? She thought about someone who knew the neighborhood, the routines, the blind spots. Someone who understood exactly where people looked and where they didn't.

Then she thought of Greg.

And all those cameras.

Her posture straightened a little.

"The strip mall," she said.

"What about it?"

"If Mark met someone there or picked something up there, there might be cameras. Store cameras. Parking lot cameras. Something."

Then Tara said, "Okay, that's actually smart."

"I know."

"Don't get cocky. It's weird on you."

Maddie smiled despite herself.

Because this, at least, was movement. A direction that wasn't just them staring at notes and making increasingly unhinged guesses.

"If we can place him," she said, "or connect that package to something real..."

"You think that's enough?"

"No," Maddie said honestly. "But I think it's more than we have now."

The back gate rattled softly.

Maddie froze.

Not loudly. Not dramatically.

Just enough.

Her head snapped toward the sound.

The yard beyond the patio stayed dark and still.

"Maddie?" Tara's voice came sharper now. "What was that?"

She stood slowly, every nerve suddenly awake. "I don't know."

The gate didn't move again.

Joon, who had followed her out at some point and settled near the door, was already up now, ears alert, body still.

Maddie's pulse thudded hard in her throat.

Maybe it was the wind.

Maybe it was nothing.

But nothing didn't feel like this.

She took one step back toward the house.

Then another.

"Maddie."

"I'm going inside," she whispered.

"Good."

She grabbed the notebook and phone and moved quickly to the door, Joon close behind her. Once inside, she locked it, then checked it twice for no reason other than her hands needed something to do.

Kent appeared at the top of the stairs, frowning. "Everything okay?"

Maddie looked up at him, breathing a little too fast.

And just like that, it was a thing now.

Not theoretical. Not private.

Real.

"No," she said. Her voice came out steadier than she felt. "I don't think it is."

CHAPTER 30
TUESDAY | THE DROP

MADDIE HADN'T TOLD Tara to come, but when she pulled up to the curb at carline to say goodbye to Lennon for the day and saw her already waiting, she wasn't surprised. Tara slid into the passenger seat without Maddie even asking, shutting the door with a quiet confidence that suggested this had never really been optional.

"You are absolutely not doing this without me," she said, buckling her seatbelt. "Plus, I brought sustenance."

Maddie glanced at the bag filled to the brim with gas station delicacies. Candy? Check. Energy drinks? Check. Salty chips? Check. They weren't quite sure how long this stakeout was going to last, and she was impressed at how prepared Tara came.

Maddie's hands stayed on the steering wheel, her eyes already scanning the street ahead. They pulled up in front of the house in the same spot as before. Far enough to be inconspicuous, but close enough to watch.

The girls gossiped about all things carline, about what Piper was wearing today, and how Maddie was liking Lennon's new therapist. Nearly two hours had passed, and they were running out of food.

That's when they saw it, Mark's truck pulled up and parked under the same oak tree as before, angled just slightly away from the curb like he hadn't planned on staying long.

They didn't fill the silence. The neighborhood moved around them like any other day. Cars passing, a dog barking somewhere in the distance, a couple walking past without a second glance. It all felt too normal as they waited for Mark to make a move.

Maddie checked the time. 10:44.

A minute later, Mark stepped out of his truck. There was no urgency in the way he moved, no hesitation either. He reached into the backseat and pulled out a small brown paper bag, folding the top once before closing the door behind him.

Maddie leaned forward slightly, her focus sharpening.

"That's not a delivery," she said.

"No," Tara agreed. "That's DiGiorno."

An eyeroll. "That's a drop."

They watched as he walked to the same mailbox, glancing once over his shoulder before opening it. The movement was quick but controlled, practiced in a way that didn't feel accidental. He placed the bag inside the mailbox and closed its lid, turning back toward his truck without lingering.

Maddie shifted her hand to the ignition. The engine turned over softly.

"Wait. What are you doing?" Tara asked.

"We're not following him this time," Maddie said. "We're staying."

That changed Tara's posture immediately. "Oh. Sneaky, sneaky."

Maddie pulled forward slowly, parking two houses down. They watched as Mark's truck disappeared around the corner, leaving the street quiet again.

The moment he was gone, Maddie opened her door.

Tara followed, her voice dropping. "This is how we die."

"We're not dying," Maddie said, trying to reassure them both, though she didn't slow down.

They walked to the mailbox together. Up close, it looked exactly like every other one on the street. Plain, unremarkable, easy to overlook. Maddie hesitated just long enough to feel the weight of what they were doing, then lifted the lid.

The paper bag sat tucked toward the back.

She pulled it out carefully and unfolded the top.

Inside were juice boxes, applesauce pouches - Ellie's favorites, a sleeve of crackers. Two cans of soup. Beneath that, travel-size shampoo, tampons.

Tara leaned in beside her, her voice softer now, "Okay."

Maddie didn't speak right away. She stared at the items, taking in the details. Nothing random. Nothing rushed. Every piece chosen with intention.

"I guess we know where Vanessa and Ellie are now," Tara said quietly.

Maddie swallowed, her eyes still on the bag. "Yep. And I don't think Mark is simply hiding them..." She shifted the contents slightly, noticing how neatly everything had been arranged. "He's taking care of them."

The realization settled between them, heavier than either of them expected.

CHAPTER 31
TUESDAY | SEEN

THEY DIDN'T LEAVE AFTER THAT.

Later, Maddie would think about that moment, the quiet shift from observation to involvement, and wonder when exactly it had happened. But standing there on the edge of the street, it didn't feel like a decision. It felt like the next logical step.

They moved back toward the car but didn't get in, instead positioning themselves just far enough away to watch without drawing attention.

"Okay," Tara said, lowering her voice. "Talk me through this."

Maddie kept her eyes on the houses, her focus narrowing. "If he's dropping supplies, they're close. Close enough that he can check on them without making it obvious."

"How close?" Tara asked.

"Walking distance," Maddie said. "Or somewhere he can get to quickly."

"Were you CIA in a past life? You're disturbingly good at this."

Maddie nodded slowly, turning her attention to the same stretch of houses. Nothing stood out at first. Everything

looked normal in that quiet, suburban way that had never felt suspicious before.

Now it did.

She scanned again, slower this time, letting her eyes settle on the edges of things instead of the obvious. That's when she saw it, a slight shift behind one of the windows.

"Did you see that?" she asked under her breath.

Tara followed her gaze. "Which one?"

"Second from the corner."

They both leaned slightly, careful not to draw attention.

The curtain moved again. Just enough.

And then...

A silhouette.

Still.

Watching.

Tara's voice dropped. "Is that..."

Maddie's breath caught before she could answer.

Vanessa.

She wasn't frantic. She wasn't pacing or hiding in the way Maddie had imagined. She stood still, composed in a way that felt almost deliberate.

Alive.

There.

Watching them.

For a moment, no one moved. The distance between them felt both too wide and not wide enough.

Then the curtain shifted again.

And she was gone.

Tara exhaled first. "Okay," she said, her voice tight. "That's not what I expected." She hesitated. "This means she didn't run."

"Or she did," Maddie said quietly. "Just not far."

A bemused chuckle.

The words didn't settle the way they should have.

Because something about what they'd just seen didn't feel right.

Vanessa hadn't looked afraid, but she hadn't looked quite free either.

CHAPTER 32
WEDNESDAY | TRUTH

MADDIE DIDN'T SLEEP much that night.

By morning, the scene had replayed in her head enough times that it felt less like a memory and more like something unfinished. Every version ended in the same place: Vanessa in the window, Mark's careful movements, the package in the mailbox, and none of it answered the question that mattered most.

Why?

Carline felt sharper the next morning, like everything had edges where it hadn't before. The same people stood in the same places, the same conversations unfolded in low, familiar tones, but Maddie noticed things differently now.

Mark was there.

Of course he was.

Same spot. Same posture. Same calm, controlled presence like nothing had shifted at all. She wondered if he knew what they saw.

Maddie watched him longer than she should have.

Tara nudged her lightly. "Subtle."

"I'm not staring," Maddie said.

"You are absolutely staring."

Maddie forced herself to look away, though it took more effort than she wanted to admit. If Mark noticed, if he connected anything, this could unravel quickly.

"Do you think he knows?" Tara asked.

"What, that we saw her?"

"Yes..."

"Only if she told him."

After drop-off, they didn't linger.

No coffee. No small talk. No pretending.

They drove straight back to the same street.

The house looked the same in daylight. It was quiet, ordinary, nothing to suggest what they had seen the night before.

"Okay," Tara said, folding her arms. "Now what?"

Maddie stared at the front door. "We talk to her."

Tara blinked. "We what?"

"We're not getting answers from Mark," Maddie said. "And we're not getting them by guessing."

"That feels like a terrible idea."

"It's the only one we have."

"Ummmm... Call the police?" Tara questioned.

"She's our friend," Maddie retorted.

"Not really..." Tara hesitated, then sighed. "Cool. Love this for us."

They walked up together, their pace measured but steady. Maddie knocked once, then again, the sound louder than it should have been in the quiet morning air.

For a second, nothing happened.

Then, footsteps.

Soft. Controlled.

The door opened just a few inches.

Vanessa stood there.

Up close, she looked different than she had in the window.

Tired, yes, but composed. Her eyes moved between them, assessing, calculating.

"You shouldn't be here," she said.

Her tone wasn't sharp. It wasn't panicked. It was certain.

Maddie held her gaze. "We know," she said as she shoved a handful of activity books and markers for Ellie into Vanessa's hands.

Vanessa didn't ask what they knew.

She didn't need to.

Her shoulders lowered slightly, something in her posture shifting from guarded to resigned.

"Thank you, but you should leave," she said.

Maddie shook her head. "We're not here for him."

That caught her attention.

Vanessa studied her for a moment longer. "Then what are you here for?"

Maddie didn't hesitate. "The truth."

CHAPTER 33
WEDNESDAY | CONFESS

VANESSA DIDN'T OPEN the door fully at first. She stood there, considering them, her hand resting against the frame like she could close it again at any moment.

Finally, she stepped back.

"Five minutes," she said. "It might not be safe."

They didn't argue, but her choice of words put an edge of fear in them.

Inside, the house felt temporary in a way Maddie couldn't fully explain. Not empty, not abandoned, but not lived in either. A bag sat near the couch, partially unzipped. A blanket was folded neatly over the armrest. Ellie's things were placed carefully nearby, each item positioned with intention.

Vanessa remained standing, so Maddie and Tara did too.

"You shouldn't have come," she said.

"We weren't going to figure it out any other way," Maddie replied.

Vanessa exhaled slowly, then nodded once. "Okay. Then listen."

Maddie didn't interrupt as she began.

"He wasn't supposed to come over that night," Vanessa said. "Derek."

There was no emotion in the way she said his name. Just fact.

"He showed up anyway."

Maddie felt Tara shift beside her, but didn't look.

"He knew things. About my ex. About everything."

The room seemed to tighten around that.

"He was using it. To keep me quiet. Like my past was nothing more than a means to an end."

Maddie's chest tightened.

Blackmail.

"He said he found him," Vanessa added. "That he would tell him where we were. But none of that mattered as much as me keeping Ellie safe."

Her voice remained steady, but her hands clenched slightly at her sides. "I believed him. Or, at the very least, I couldn't risk that he was telling the truth."

Maddie understood why. "So what happened?" she asked gently.

Vanessa hesitated, then continued. "I tried to talk to him rationally, parent to parent, but it wasn't getting through to him. He was getting more and more agitated. The only thing he seemed to care about was the consequences he would face."

"With the financial stuff? The stealing?"

"Yes. But Mark heard us. He lives next door. He came over when things got loud."

That tracked.

"He tried to get Derek to leave. But Derek wouldn't stop. He kept pushing. Kept talking. Kept threatening." Maddie could see the fear in Vanessa's face. Her jaw tightened. "And then..." tears started flowing down Vanessa's cheeks.

She didn't describe it, but she didn't need to.

Maddie could see it clearly enough.

A moment. A shift. Something that couldn't be undone.

"After," Vanessa said, her voice quieter now, "Mark told

me to leave. Said it wasn't safe. That if anyone found out… I didn't want to risk it. Didn't want to risk Ellie. Mark told us where to go, told us we'd be safe."

Maddie nodded slowly. "And you believed him."

Vanessa met her gaze. "Yes. He's been looking out for us since the day we moved to Dogwood Bay. But at this point, I don't know if we'll ever get to go home."

A beat passed between them.

Then Maddie asked the question that had been building since the night before. "Do you still? Trust him?"

Vanessa didn't answer immediately. Her eyes flicked toward the window, toward the street beyond it, toward everything waiting outside. Finally, she said, "I don't know."

And that uncertainty settled heavier than anything else she had said.

CHAPTER 34
WEDNESDAY | CONFRONT

THEY DIDN'T SAY much after they left the house.

Maddie walked back to the car with a steady pace, her thoughts moving faster than she could organize them. Tara stayed close beside her, unusually quiet for once, like she was still catching up to everything they had just heard.

Inside the car, Maddie closed the door and sat there for a moment, her hands resting on the steering wheel without turning the engine on.

"Well," Tara said finally, exhaling. "That was... a lot."

Maddie nodded. "Yeah."

Neither of them moved.

Because now they knew.

Not pieces. Not theories. Not assumptions.

The truth.

"Okay," Tara said, turning slightly in her seat. "So what are we doing with that?"

Maddie stared out the windshield, her mind replaying Vanessa's words. Derek. The threat. Mark stepping in. The moment everything shifted.

"Based on what Vanessa said, he didn't mean to kill him," she said quietly.

"No," Tara agreed. "But he still did. He's our murderer."

Maddie nodded again, slower this time.

"And now he's covering it up," Tara added. "Which feels... less accidental."

"The question is, is he covering it up to keep Vanessa safe... or himself? What's really at play here?"

That part sat heavier.

Maddie finally turned the key in the ignition. The engine came to life, grounding the moment just enough to move forward.

"We talk to him," she said.

Tara blinked. "We are just... doing that now?"

"Talking to a murderer? We already crossed the line. We don't get to pretend we didn't."

Tara let out a short breath. "Cool. Love that we've fully committed to this life."

They didn't drive far.

Mark's truck was exactly where it always was this time of day, parked near The Pretty Petal. The shop windows reflected the late afternoon light, soft and warm in a way that didn't match the weight sitting in Maddie's chest.

Inside, the shop was quiet.

Something about coming while it was still daylight out made it feel less creepy. Like it was safer somehow.

Mark stood behind the counter, trimming stems with the same careful precision Maddie had seen before. He looked up when the door chimed, his expression shifting just slightly when he saw them.

"Maddie," he said. "Tara."

"Hey," Maddie replied.

For a moment, no one spoke.

The air felt different now. Not tense exactly, but aware.

Mark set the shears down slowly. "What can I help you with?"

"The arrangements at the service were beautiful," Maddie started. "I figured you did most of them."

Tara, however, didn't ease into it. "We saw her."

A flicker.

Small.

But there.

Mark didn't ask who.

He didn't need to.

His jaw tightened just enough to notice. "You shouldn't have gone there."

"That's not really the point anymore," Tara replied. "She's our friend, and we needed to know that she was safe."

Mark's eyes shifted to her briefly, then back to Maddie.

"She told us about that night, about what happened," Maddie continued.

Another pause.

Longer this time.

Mark leaned back slightly against the counter, crossing his arms. Not defensive. Not open either. Just... steady.

"And what exactly do you think happened?" he asked.

Maddie held his gaze. "That you heard him threatening her. Stepped in. And then something went wrong."

Silence filled the space between them.

Mark didn't look away. A nod, but it wasn't paired with an admission of guilt.

He didn't interrupt, letting them continue to work out their theory.

"We don't think it was planned," Tara added. "But everything after… was."

"We just don't understand why. Why is Vanessa hiding? Why haven't you told the truth?"

Mark exhaled slowly, calm, running a hand along the back of his neck. "He wasn't going to stop," he said finally. "You didn't hear the way he was talking to her."

Maddie didn't respond.

Because she believed that part.

"He knew exactly what he was doing. He knew what that threat meant."

"Her ex?" Maddie asked.

"He did bad things, really bad things. Vanessa had turned their life around. She was still on high alert about everyone and everything, but she was learning how to trust again."

That explained the notebook.

His voice stayed controlled, but there was something under it now. Not anger. Not quite. Something closer to frustration that hadn't gone anywhere.

"I didn't go over there to hurt him," he said, *almost* apologetically. "I went over there to make him leave."

"And?" Tara asked.

Mark's gaze shifted, just slightly, like he was looking at something that wasn't in the room anymore. "And he didn't."

A beat.

"That's all it took," Tara said quietly.

"Took…" A scoff. "That bastard took from me, from Lindsay, from Ryan, from damn near everyone. But that was just money. He was going to take so much more from Vanessa."

Maddie stepped a little closer. Understanding the depth of what Mark just said. "You told her to run."

He nodded once. "I thought Derek had maybe already told her ex where she was. I had to be sure. We had a plan in place long before Derek showed up; he just forced us to put it in motion. She needed to be out of there before anyone showed up. Before this turned into something worse."

CHAPTER 35
WEDNESDAY | EXPOSURE

THE SHOP FELT SMALLER after that.

Not physically, but in the way everything seemed to narrow around what Mark had just said.

Maddie studied him more carefully now, looking past the version of him she thought she knew. "What do you mean?"

Mark hesitated, like he was weighing something. Then he made a decision. "He's out."

Tara frowned. "Who is?"

"Her ex. Eric. He's been in prison, but was released last month."

The words landed hard.

Maddie felt it immediately, the way the pieces started to shift into a different shape.

"Vanessa was sent an alert and has been focused on keeping a low profile and paying attention to everyone and everything ever since."

"I take it… you're not just... a florist," Maddie said.

A small, humorless smile pulled at the corner of his mouth. "I am. This is just quieter."

Tara stared at him. "You're kidding."

"I'm not."

The room went still.

Maddie's thoughts moved quickly now, reorganizing everything she had assumed about him. "You knew about Vanessa before any of this."

Mark nodded. "I knew enough to know she wasn't just being *dramatic*."

"And Derek found out."

"Yeah. And decided to use it."

The anger was clearer now.

Not explosive.

Controlled.

"He thought it was leverage," Mark continued. "Something he could hold over her to keep his own situation from blowing up."

"The fraud," Tara said matter-of-factly.

Mark nodded once, then looked back at Maddie. "I didn't plan any of it. But once it happened... I wasn't going to let her take the fall for it. Not with him out there."

Maddie felt that settle. "You hid her."

"I kept her somewhere safe," he corrected.

"And the drops?"

"Supplies," he said simply. "So she doesn't have to be seen. I was figuring out a plan."

Maddie thought of the bag. The careful choices. The routine. "You're watching the house."

"Trying to make sure no one else is."

Tara crossed her arms. "Including us."

"You sent the text, didn't you?" Maddie questioned.

Mark didn't deny it.

Silence stretched between them again, but it felt different now. Not uncertain. Not confused.

Clear.

"You should've told the police," Maddie said.

Mark shook his head. "And say what? That I killed him? That she ran because of something no one's supposed to know about? Her past destroyed her once. It wasn't fair for her to be victimized all over again."

"But," Tara said. "You could have come clean."

Mark looked at her evenly. "And then what happens when her ex finds out where she is? And I'm not around to protect her?"

That stopped her.

Because there wasn't a clean answer.

Maddie exhaled slowly. "So what's your plan?"

Mark didn't hesitate this time. "Keep her safe until he's back in custody."

"And if he's not?" Tara asked.

Mark's expression didn't change. "Then we figure out the next step."

Maddie studied him for a long moment.

Because for the first time, this didn't feel like a mystery anymore.

It felt like a decision.

CHAPTER 36

THURSDAY | VANISHED

CARLINE FELT off before anything even happened.

Maddie noticed it as soon as she pulled in. Nothing looked different on the surface. The same line of cars curved along the curb, parents stood half-engaged in conversation, and kids shuffled forward in uneven lines of backpacks and noise. But something underneath it all felt tighter, like the movement of the day was just slightly out of sync.

Tara must have felt it, too. She didn't start with a joke or a comment, just leaned against the side of Maddie's car and scanned the line with narrowed eyes.

"You feel that?" she asked quietly.

Maddie nodded. "Yeah."

Before either of them could say more, Mark approached.

That alone was enough to shift everything.

He didn't come to them like this. Not directly, not in the open, not during carline, where eyes were everywhere. His expression was controlled, but there was something underneath it that Maddie hadn't seen before. Not panic, but something close to it.

"Hey," he said, stopping just short of them.

"Hey," Maddie replied, her voice steady even as her attention sharpened.

Tara straightened beside her. "You're breaking routine. I don't like it."

She expected a slight grin, but Mark didn't react, instead he asked, "When was the last time you saw her?"

Maddie didn't pretend not to understand. "Yesterday morning. At the house."

Mark nodded once, like he had expected that answer. "She missed two check-ins."

The words landed hard, settling into Maddie's chest before she could fully process them.

"What does that mean?" Tara asked, her voice quieter now.

"It means she's not where she's supposed to be," Mark said. "We talk twice a day on a burner; she hasn't picked up either call."

Concern.

The noise of carline continued around them, but it felt distant, like it was happening somewhere else entirely.

"I went by this morning," he said. "Didn't go in. Didn't want to draw attention."

Maddie didn't hesitate. "Then let's go now."

Tara blinked, turning toward her. "We are just... leaving?"

"Yes," Maddie said, already reaching for her keys.

There wasn't time to overthink it. Not now.

The drive was quiet, the kind of silence that wasn't comfortable but necessary. Mark followed behind them, his truck steady in Maddie's rearview mirror. No one spoke, because they were all thinking the same thing and none of them wanted to say it out loud.

When they pulled up to the house, the shift was immediate.

Nothing looked wrong.

And that was the problem.

The door was closed. The curtains were still. The house sat exactly as it had before, but the stillness didn't feel controlled anymore. It felt hollow.

Maddie walked up first, knocking once before trying the handle. Mark started to move around to the back.

"Unlocked!" Maddie whisper-shouted.

She pushed the door open slowly, her chest heaving and contracting with every breath. They stepped inside.

The room was empty.

Not quiet in the way it had been before, not carefully maintained or intentionally sparse. Empty in a way that felt abrupt, like something had been removed all at once.

The bag by the couch was gone. The blanket. Ellie's things.

Everything.

Tara stepped in behind her, her voice low. "Okay. That's not good."

Mark moved past them, scanning the room quickly, his focus sharper now. "No signs of a struggle."

Maddie turned slowly, taking in the space again. No overturned furniture. No broken glass. No obvious disturbance.

Just absence.

"They didn't leave like this," she said quietly.

"No," Mark agreed. "She wouldn't."

Tara crossed her arms, her expression tightening. "So what, someone just walked in and took them?"

No one answered.

Because they all knew who that someone was.

CHAPTER 37
THURSDAY | FOUND

MADDIE'S PHONE rang before she even made it back to the car.

She glanced at the screen.

Greg.

She answered immediately. "Greg?"

"I need you to come over," he said. "Now."

Her stomach dropped. "Why?"

"I caught something on the cameras last night. You need to see it."

She didn't ask anything else. "We're on our way."

The drive felt shorter than it should have, the tension in the car thick enough to make the silence feel heavy. By the time they reached Greg's house, he had already pulled the footage up, the screen glowing in the dim light of his living room.

He gave a nod to the trio as they entered and approached the computer.

"Watch," he said, stepping aside.

Maddie moved closer as the video played.

Vanessa's house.

Dark.

Still.

Then movement.

A figure approached from the side, partially obscured by shadow but moving with purpose. Not Derek. Not Mark. Someone else.

The door opened. Closed.

Then nothing.

Minutes passed on the screen, stretching longer than they should have.

Tara leaned forward slightly. "That's him."

Mark didn't respond right away, but something in his posture changed. "That's Eric."

"I called the police," Greg said in a panicked voice. "They said what I saw might be suspicious, but it didn't mean a crime was taking place. I told them... I told them I know the house, the family, the neighborhood, but they didn't listen. Said they couldn't even do a wellness check since Vanessa and Ellie were still in the wind. Just told me they'd swing by on their shift... Whatever that means."

"Stay here," Mark said.

Maddie didn't.

Neither did Tara.

Greg obeyed.

The three of them, Mark, Maddie, and Tara, crossed the street to Vanessa's house. From the outside, nothing appeared different, but in her bones, Maddie felt that something was deeply, deeply wrong.

Maddie and Tara acted as Mark's shadow, stepping onto the front porch with intention. Maddie could see the anger and fear in Mark's face. She found herself wondering, *Just how bad of a guy is this Eric?*

"I'm going to open this door," Mark stated. "Find Vanessa

and Ellie, and pray they are safe. If you see anyone else, anyone at all, scream." It was not a request, but a demand.

The door was locked, but not for long. Mark forced it open with a controlled hit, stepping inside without breaking stride. A firm hand on his gun.

The air inside felt wrong immediately. Stale. Heavy.

Then a sound.

Faint.

From down the hall.

Mark moved first, fast and focused, in a way Maddie hadn't seen before. He reached the door at the end, pushed it open.

Vanessa and Ellie were inside.

Tied.

Crying.

But alive.

Ellie let out a gasp the second she saw them. Vanessa's expression shifted all at once, relief breaking through the control she had been holding onto.

"He's still here," she whispered. Dryness in her throat. "He's still here. I knew he'd find us..."

Maddie moved forward immediately, dropping to her knees beside them, working quickly to untie their hands. "You're okay," she said, her voice steadier than she felt.

Vanessa nodded, pulling Ellie close the second she was free, then screamed, "Behind you!"

Eric was fast, but Mark was faster.

As Eric lunged into the bedroom, Mark was already on him.

Tara helped Vanessa to shelter Ellie under their bodies. Not wanting her to see what was happening in the chaos around them. Truth be told, she didn't want to see it either.

The movement was fast, controlled, decisive. There was

no chaos to it, no hesitation. Within seconds, Eric was on the ground, restrained, and any chance of escape gone.

Mark stood, pulling out his phone.

"It's over," he said.

And this time, it actually was.

CHAPTER 38
FRIDAY | AGAIN

CARLINE LOOKED EXACTLY THE SAME.

That was the strangest part.

After everything, the questions, the patterns, the notebook, the day that could have ended very differently, nothing about the outside world had shifted at all.

Cars lined up along the curb. Parents stood in loose clusters, talking about things that didn't matter in the way they had mattered before. Kids moved in uneven lines, backpacks bouncing, voices carrying across the lot.

Normal.

Tara leaned against Maddie's car, coffee in hand, her posture relaxed in a way it hadn't been all week, and an energy drink extended in Maddie's direction.

"So," she said, glancing over. "That escalated."

Maddie accepted the drink and let out a quiet laugh. "A little."

Across the lot, Mark stood in his usual spot.

But not really.

He wasn't watching the way he had been before. Not tracking. Not calculating.

Just standing there.

Present.

The weight he had been carrying hadn't disappeared, but it had shifted into something else. Something resolved.

Eric was in custody.

Mark had told the police everything.

He told them about what led to Derek being at Vanessa's. About Eric being released. About the phone threats she received and his plan to keep them safe.

And then, he told them about how he pushed Derek backward in an attempt to get him to leave, how he fell and smashed his head on the corner of the counter. How he dragged the body outside so they didn't risk Ellie seeing it.

And most importantly, Vanessa and Ellie were finally home, no longer looking over their shoulders or waiting for the next thing to go wrong. For the first time in a long time, their lives felt steady.

Mark was expected to be charged with involuntary manslaughter, but between his clean record, his stellar time with the force in St. Louis, the circumstances surrounding Derek's death, and his full cooperation with law enforcement, it was unlikely he would serve any jail time. What happened that night hadn't been planned, and everyone involved knew it.

Eric, on the other hand, was charged with armed kidnapping. With his history of violence and now a far more serious offense, no one expected to see him out for a very long time.

Tara followed Maddie's gaze. "You realize we accidentally helped solve a murder and stop a kidnapping."

"I'm pretty sure it was intentional," Maddie said.

"We are total bad-asses."

"We are kind of cool, aren't we?" Maddie smiled slightly, her attention drifting back to the line.

For the first time in a while, she wasn't analyzing what she saw. She wasn't looking for patterns or inconsistencies or anything that didn't fit.

She was just watching.

Lennon stepped out of the building a few minutes later, his backpack bouncing as Miss Merissa walked him toward the car, completely unaware of how close his mom had come to danger.

"You think we're done?" Tara asked.

Maddie considered that, her gaze moving across the familiar scene.

All the things they had missed before they started paying attention.

All the things still happening, unnoticed.

She shook her head slightly. "I think we just learned how much we don't see."

Tara smiled at that, a small spark of something already returning. "Cool. So we're definitely doing this again."

Maddie exhaled, the tension finally easing out of her chest. "Maybe."

But this time, it didn't feel like a maybe at all.

A NOTE FROM THE AUTHOR

Thank you so much for reading *Snacks, Schedules, and Everyone's a Suspect*. I hope you enjoyed spending time with Maddie and Tara as much as I enjoyed creating their world.

If I'm being honest, writing this book probably should not have fit into my life. My schedule already leaves very little to the imagination, and there were definitely moments where I neglected things that probably should not have been neglected in order to write. Somehow, between teaching, parenting, marketing deadlines, household chaos, and an unhealthy dependence on iced caffeine, this story still found its way onto the page.

Over the years, I've worked with news outlets, nonprofits, schools, museums, and more. While I loved much of that work and many of the incredible people I met along the way, I often found myself jealous of people who seemed to have "found their calling" or always knew exactly what they wanted to be.

That was never me.

Then, in 2025, I rediscovered reading, and it completely consumed me in the best way. Books became part of my daily life and identity, and somewhere along the way, reading turned into writing. I may still be finding my voice as an author, but this is the first thing in a very long time that has felt entirely mine.

The Carline Cozy Mysteries are just getting started, and I already have more chaos, gossip, suspects, and questionable decision-making planned for this series.

Thank you again for supporting indie authors and spending your time with my stories. It means more than you know.

ABOUT THE AUTHOR

Kristin Elizabeth is the author of the Carline Cozy Mysteries (so far, just the one book), where carline chaos, caffeine, gossip, and crumb-covered minivans collide with clues, secrets, and murder investigations. By day, she is an autism teacher and by night, a freelance digital marketing and content manager, balancing lesson plans, deadlines, and family life with her caffeine dependence.

She holds a Master's degree in Special Education with an Autism focus and another in Entertainment Business, bringing both professional experience and personal insight into the worlds she creates.

As a mom to a neurodivergent child, Kristin brings humor, heart, and an authentic perspective to the messy realities of motherhood, friendship, and finding yourself again somewhere between the school pickup line and survival mode.

When she's not writing, Kristin can usually be found reading cozy mysteries and thrillers, building brands, or plotting fictional crimes while waiting in carline.

Connect with her here:

🌐 kristinelizabethauthor.com

📚 Instagram: @kristinelizabethauthor

ALSO BY KRISTIN ELIZABETH

Petals & Poison | A Beatrix Hawthorne Mystery

Coming Fall 2026

When a member of Rowanridge's magical community is found dead during reunion festivities, Earth Witch Beatrix Hawthorne finds herself tangled in a murder investigation rooted in old friendships, buried rivalries, and dangerous secrets. Between running her family flower shop, navigating complicated relationships, and trying not to become the next victim, Bea quickly learns that in a town built on magic, almost everyone has something to hide.

Perfect for readers who love cozy mysteries with witchy small-town vibes, layered friendships, found family, and a touch of romance.

Prombie

Coming Winter 2026

Sloane Hart was supposed to have the perfect prom night. Instead, she woke up dead… and hungry.

Unfortunately for Sloane, being resurrected is not subtle. Her skin is gray, and no amount of lip gloss can hide the fact that she is visibly the walking dead.

Now stuck somewhere between prom queen and actual monster, Sloane is forced to figure out who she really is beneath the mascara and social climbing. Between her increasingly questionable appetite and a growing number of missing classmates, senior year is literally falling apart.

Campy, chaotic, bloody, and weirdly heartfelt, *Prombie* is a dark rom-com horror about identity, obsession, terrible choices, and becoming more human after death than you ever managed to be while alive.